LOCKDOWN

JANNA THOMPSON

Clan Destine
PRESS

First published by Clan Destine Press in 2022

Clan Destine Press
PO Box 121, Bittern
Victoria, 3918 Australia

National Library of Australia Cataloguing-In-Publication data:

Thompson, Janna

Lockdown

ISBN: 978-1-922904-20-1   (paperback)
ISBN: 978-1-922904-21-8   (eBook)

Cover Design by © Willsin Rowe

Design & Typesetting by Clan Destine Press

Clan Destine
P R E S S

www.clandestinepress.net

CHAPTER 1

Jenny

A DIM LIGHT, A DULL NOISE IN THE DISTANCE AND THERE SHE IS. BUT where? She is floating through a grey mist until her eyes focus on cracks in the wall. The plaster between them balloons outward, like a flower, reminding her of the lilies that once grew in her garden.

I'm Jenny. My name is Jennifer Mueller.

A trolley clanks and the door opens.

'Good morning, Mrs Mueller. Did you sleep well?'

It is Nancy with breakfast. Nancy slides the tray onto a table in front of the bed. 'It's porridge and a nice glass of apple juice.'

Jenny looks at the grey mass on the plate.

'Do you want me to help?' Nancy doesn't wait for an answer, bustling to the window to open the blinds. It is bright outside but only sky is visible.

Jenny remembers she is at Sunnyvale. But where is Sara? She urgently wants to talk to Sara but she does not dare call out, or try to get up. The man will come if she makes a fuss.

Nancy smiles. 'Your son Colin is coming today. Won't that be nice?'

Jenny eats most of the bland porridge. The tray is removed and Nancy leaves her looking out the window. A bird flits past – too quickly to see what type.

She closes her eyes and sees a familiar room furnished with a couch and two armchairs.

I am Jenny Mueller and this is where I live.

She drifts through the room; it's tidy – just as she left it. There is a dictionary on the coffee table. Neil likes word games. Above the couch is a picture of the Hebrides. He says it reminds him of his childhood in Scotland. In a corner is a portrait of her aunt her face frozen in a condescending smile. How did that get here? The picture makes her uneasy and she drifts away.

A voice comes from the hallway. 'Jenny, did you get pumpkin for the soup?' Neil's voice, but he can't be here. He died two – no three – years ago.

She finds herself in the kitchen. All the food, dishes and utensils have been cleared, the bench wiped clean. A calendar hangs on the wall, but the dates are obscured. Something out of place catches her attention. The rubbish bin is overflowing with of old clothes.

Why didn't I empty it?

She sees a grey sleeve hanging over the side. A button is missing and there is a red stain on the fabric.

She wants to scream, but no sound comes.

'Breathe slowly. Take deep strong breaths,' says Sara.

The house has gone, Sara is beside her on their favourite park bench.

'Lean against me and breathe deeply.'

Jenny hugs her friend and closes her eyes. The advice works. Calmer, Jenny opens her eyes. The lake is not blood red as she feared, and the birds in the trees are not carrion crows.

'I'm sorry.'

'Relax,' says Sara. 'We can stay here. We don't have to move.'

Sara is wearing a light blue dress, which complements her dark brown hair. A large scarf is wrapped around her neck and shoulders, a red handbag beside her on the bench.

'I was so frightened. I couldn't help it.'

Sara holds her tighter.

'I think about it all the time. I keep seeing her blood.' She takes a deep breath. 'I must know.'

'Yes?' Sara leans back, their hands retaining the contact.

'I need to know what happened to my mother.'

Jenny knows there is more to that desperation.

Did I kill her?

The silence on the bench drags until Sara releases Jenny's hand.

'I have an idea which might help.'

Jenny turns to Sara.

'Write down everything that happened in the days before your mother was killed. What people said and did, including yourself. But don't describe it from your viewpoint. Do it as if another person saw and heard everything. Does that make sense?'

Jenny nods. 'It's telling what happened from the outside.'

'Yes. It puts distance between you and traumatic events, and helps you concentrate on what happened around you.' Sara pauses. 'Can you do this?'

Another nod.

'Don't do it if it causes pain.'

Jenny acknowledges the concern but already knows Sara's suggestion might help her find the answers. She will buy note paper on the way home.

Footsteps echo in a corridor; Sara is gone and Jenny is back in her room at Sunnyvale. Nancy is talking to someone outside the door. A man replies and Jenny braces herself. It's futile, she can't stop what is going to happen.

The door opens and a large man dressed in white enters.

She pushes against the headboard as Harry approaches with the loaded syringe.. She considers striking the arm pinning her against the pillow. It's useless to resist, they'll tie her down if she kicks or screams.

Harry's breath smells of peppermint. She used to like that smell but not anymore.

The needle slides into her arm.

CHAPTER 2

Meg

'It's not that she has bruises or any other sign of abuse. But she's frightened. She has moments when she shakes with fear, and her eyes – they look like she's seen something terrible. Or that something terrible has been done to her. But when we ask her what's wrong she just shakes her head.'

A serviette delivered with the coffee was shredded as Mr Brighouse talked.

We were sitting in the back room of a café in the business end of the city. Dorothy had her notebook on the table. 'Do you remember when you first noticed her fear?'

'We visited the nursing home on her birthday a month ago, Mrs Arden. It was March 8. She was in such a state that she hardly noticed the presents we brought.' He paused while Dorothy wrote. 'We had dinner reservations, but she was too frightened to leave her room. She kept saying that she couldn't talk to us.'

The son deeply concerned about his 85-year-old mother was himself elderly. Mr Brighouse was tall, his knees barely fitted under the table. He had once been handsome but jowls reflected the battle with age and gravity. A career of worrying about profit and loss had lined his face. A obvious source of pride was a thick head of stylish white hair.

Lila brushed crumbs off the table. 'Did you question the staff?'

'Yes, of course, Mrs Gatti.'

A self-satisfied smile. He was a businessman who loved showing his ability to remember new acquaintance's names.

'I questioned the nurses, the supervisor, even the cleaner. They don't know anything..' He crumpled the serviette and threw it on the table.

Mrs Brighouse patted his hand. She was at least a decade younger with a much better figure. Light brown hair, dyed, to be sure, framed a heavily made-up face that could still be described as pretty.

'The manager told us her anxiety is one of the effects of dementia,' Mrs Brighouse said. 'They're giving her some medication.' She sounded impatient, indicating that further investigation was a waste of time.

Her expression had been dubious since entering the cafe with her husband. I could guess what she was thinking: why would anyone want help from three elderly women?

Mr Brighouse took his hand away. 'It's not just anxiety. It's fear.'

'Can she communicate?' I asked. 'Has she been able to tell you anything that might be helpful? '

Mr Brighouse looked at me with a puzzled expression, as if he hadn't noticed my presence. I realised that his ability to remember names had failed him.

'Meg Thorne.'

'Of course, Mrs Thorne. The retired philosophy professor.' He seemed to find the idea amusing. 'Yes, Mrs Thorne, she's able to talk. She's not that far gone into dementia. Mostly she talks about her childhood in England. Until recently she was willing to tell us about her daily life, the people she meets for a cup of tea, and so on. Now, when we ask her questions about her activities, she just stares into space.'

I wanted to find out more about this woman who had become such a worry for her son. 'What's her name?'

'Sara. Sara Brighouse. She and my father came to Australia after the War. They settled in Hampstead. We're a Hampstead family.'

Lila nodded slowly, as if she agreed that this was a fine thing.

Dorothy raised her eyebrows at me. Then she tapped her notebook with her pencil. 'How about the other residents? Did you notice anything disturbing in the way the staff treated them?'

She was expressing a shared suspicion. A government inquiry into the treatment of nursing homes residents revealed horrible cases of abuse.

Witnesses described homes where dementia sufferers were strapped to their beds, left unattended for hours in their bodily wastes, or were over-medicated to make them docile. Patients were found with bruises from rough handling, and in some nursing homes, staff got away with sexual abuse and sadistic behaviour.

Mr Brighouse raised his hand to object to Dorothy's suggestion. 'No, she's in the Sunnyvale Residential and Care Home in Hampstead. It's got an excellent reputation. It was set up with money from Mrs Josephine Wakefield's charitable foundation. Mrs Wakefield lives there herself and she's not a woman to let things slide. We've never seen any reason to be concerned. The place is very well run.'

He took a brochure from a folder and handed it to me. I noted the cover featured a modern brick building next door to a park, then passed it to Lila.

'It's also expensive,' said Mrs Brighouse. 'Mrs Wakefield's money is invested there, but it's no charity.'

Mrs Wakefield was the charity queen of Melbourne. She often featured in newspapers and on television at the openings of hospital wings, hospices and care homes to which her large fortune had contributed. She was famous when I arrived in the country almost sixty years ago and would be about the same age as Mr Brighouse's mother.

'Could someone be bullying her?' I asked. 'Another resident, perhaps?'

He shrugged. 'The staff insist that nothing like that is happening. Personally, I think it's the most likely explanation. My mother is a timid woman. It wouldn't be difficult for someone to frighten her. We've thought of moving her somewhere else. But she's used to Sunnyvale and a friend of hers, a woman named Jenny Mueller, is there, though unfortunately her dementia is even worse.'

He was anxious to get to the point of our meeting. 'My lawyer and I agree that the best idea is to get someone inside to investigate. We think that one of you could become a resident – for a temporary period of course.' He looked directly at me.

I was not happy to be singled out as the most likely candidate for a nursing home. It's true I am the oldest and frailest member of our group, but I had no intention of taking up residence at Sunnyvale or any other care home.

'We will pay. You'll have to come up with a story about why you're being admitted for a short term stay. We can leave the details to you. My lawyer says that you ladies have worked with him before. He highly recommends you.' His voice rose at the end, as if he couldn't work out how that could be true.

We were, in fact, an unlikely team of private investigators. Lila, now adjusting the purple gown that stretched over her ample bosom and patting the beret that bore down on, but could not control, a head of curly grey hair, must have looked to this carefully dressed businessman like a hippy matriarch. Dorothy, tall and angular, with her prominent nose and severe expression, could have been a model for a statue at Easter Island. And I, sitting in the corner, a diminutive, wispy figure, was dressed in the unassuming pastel colours often favoured by elderly ladies.

Mr Brighouse began the work of untangling his legs from beneath the table. His wife was already on her feet, handbag under her arm, eager to depart.

'Of course,' she said, 'it's likely to be nothing more than what they think – dementia. We just need to be sure.' She could not make it clearer that she thought that an investigation by three elderly women was a waste of time and money.

Mr Brighouse stopped at the café door. 'My lawyer, Mr Todd, told me you were the ladies who helped him force that charlatan Wilde to pay out a lot of money to his victims.' His smiled, 'Who would have thought?'

Yes, I said to myself, who would have thought?

He nodded. 'Nice to meet you, ladies. I look forward to getting your report.

CHAPTER 3

Meg

DOROTHY PICKED UP THE CARE HOME BROCHURE.

'It says Sunnyvale offers luxury accommodation in peaceful surroundings with activities to suit any preference or level of mobility as well as top class facilities, including a hairdresser and a gymnasium. The food, "is cooked by an award-winning chef" – whatever that means. And it's able to offer services for those with special needs and hospital care.' She turned to me. 'Aren't you tempted, Meg?' The brochure was passed to Lila.

'No.' I crossed my arms; I wasn't going to be persuaded.

Lila looked at the cover photo. 'I've heard about Sunnyvale but I can't think of the connection.'

'I hope it wasn't mentioned at the Royal Commission,' I said.

'No, I'm sure that's not it. Something I heard a long time ago.'

She shook her head and returned the brochure to the table; on the back was Josephine Wakefield. It was a copy of a portrait rather than a photograph. It showed her as a handsome woman in her 60s. She had strong features: high cheek bones, a prominent nose and penetrating blue eyes. She was smiling but her expression, it seemed to me, was judgmental rather than congenial. Was she about to find fault with a public servant or perhaps the ball gown of another society lady?

'She must be almost ninety by now,' I said. 'She can't still look like this.'

Dorothy bent over to look. 'She's the founder and patron of Sunnyvale, and lives there. Wouldn't you like to mix with high society, Meg?'

'No,' I said. The idea of going into a nursing home knotted my stomach.

'My father met her once,' said Lila. 'It was when he was the organiser of a group that helped Italian migrants find their feet in Australia. She was the queen bee, he said, dressing down for sake of the company, but wearing enough jewellery to show where she really belonged. He thought she was more concerned with making an impression than the causes of the people she talked to. But he didn't want to be too critical as she was giving money to his organisation.' She lifted her eyes from the brochure. 'Well then, what should we do to help Mr and Mrs Brighouse?'

'I didn't like them,' said Dorothy. 'They're so keen on letting us know how much they're spending on the old lady. Upper class suburb, upper class nursing home. And the wife doesn't care about her at all.'

'But *he* cares,' I said. 'Give him credit for that. And relieving the suffering of an old woman is surely a good thing to do.'

'Glad to get approval from our ethics committee.' Dorothy wanted to make a plan. 'Anyway, we've agreed to do the job, so now the only question is how we're going to manage it. Who's going to take up temporary residence at Sunnyvale?'

'You, Dorothy,' I quickly suggested. 'You're the obvious choice. You're organised and good at handling people.' Dorothy had managed a Footscray pub for many years. To me, breaking up fights, tossing out drunks and forcing everyone to leave at closing time more than qualified her for dealing with the residents and staff at Sunnyvale.

Lila's laughter filled the cafe. 'Too right. She'd threaten them with the wrath of God. They'd soon be on their knees to confess every sin they've committed. She always wanted to be a pastor in another life.'

A cup clattered on the table. The church volunteer pointed at Lila. 'All you'd have to do to is to threaten to kiss the men and to give the women a sample of your perfume.'

Lila grinned. 'They wouldn't let you in the door without a bag over your head.'

'You wouldn't be able to get through the door, you tub of lard.'

Lila patted her stomach. 'It's not lard so much as gristle.'

They laughed; Lila's startled people at the next table, Dorothy's was a low rumble at the back of her throat. I shifted uncomfortably in my chair as they turned to me.

'You're the obvious choice,' said Dorothy.

I shook my head. 'No. I'm not good at noticing things.'

Thoughts of my mother came to me.

Please don't make me go into a home. Please, no. I'll die there.

And she did. I squirmed again in the chair.

'But you'd be perfect,' Dorothy wasn't deterred. 'You can wander around listening to conversations. No one will suspect that you're spying on them.'

'Do you think I'm invisible?'

'Next best thing.' Lila said. 'You go in for self-effacement. If the police came here in a few hours and wanted the waitress to describe her customers, she would remember Dorothy and me.' She waved a hand between them.

'Mr and Mrs Brighouse were over-dressed for this place; the waitress couldn't forget them.' Lila looked around the café. 'Those mothers with their babies and strollers and that good-looking student on the computer would probably be memorable.' She turned back to me with a smile. 'But she wouldn't remember you. If you were a spy, or a criminal on the run, that would be to your advantage.'

I was about to protest – but Lila put up her hand.

'Nobody notices your beige skirts and cream coloured blouses. You put on just enough makeup to look like a proper Anglo lady of a certain age. You always sit in the corner and stay still. No one would guess that you have superpowers.'

'Superpowers?'

'Like tangling a person up in an argument so tight that he can't free himself,' said Lila.

'Or putting people to sleep by giving them a lecture on ethics,' added Dorothy. 'That criminal Wilde was no match for you. By comparison, this job is a breeze.'

'Think of it as a holiday,' added Lila. 'Like being on cruise ship without ocean views or the fear of being seasick. Same demographic too.'

I didn't see the mission in such rosy terms. I imagined being strapped to a bed with a nurse hovering over me, about to inject me with something that would make me unable to communicate. That made me think about my mother.

Please. I don't like this place. You have to get me out of here. I want to go home.

I had taken her hand and shaken my head. Her home had had to be sold when she went into care as I couldn't have looked after her by myself. What she'd most wanted had been beyond my powers.

'You won't be alone,' Lila said. 'I'll visit you – every day if you like – to make sure you're all right. You can pass me any information you uncover.'

'I know people in the catering industry,' Dorothy said. 'I might be able to find a job in the Sunnyvale kitchen or maybe as a cleaner. In any case, I'll get to know the staff. I can keep track of you..'

'There's no danger,' added Lila. 'These places aren't prisons. You can always get out or have visitors. And you have your phone in case you need help.'

'If the old Mrs Brighouse is being bullied, it shouldn't take long to find the culprit.' Dorothy smiled. 'You'll be out of there in less than a week.'

I shook my head, clasping my arms tighter.

Please, my mother begged. *Get me out of here.*

'Some people are frightened by spiders,' I told them. 'Some by heights. I can't stand the idea of being in a nursing home.' I was entitled to my phobia.

Dorothy groaned.

I turned to Lila. 'If it's like taking a cruise holiday, why shouldn't you be happy to do it?'

Lila sighed. 'There's Dan, you know.'

Her son Daniel had been seriously injured in an accident as a teenager; he couldn't walk, talk or do anything for himself. Daniel was in St Bernard's care home which visited almost every day. She said that reading gave him comfort.

I was sceptical. Lila had taken me on one of her visits. What I saw was a shapeless, unresponsive hulk under a quilt, unseeing eyes directed at the ceiling. I couldn't tell Lila that I thought her son was a human vegetable. There was no question that he was well cared for. Lila's brief absence would do him no harm, and she knew it.

We lapsed into a long silence. It was broken by the start of a news broadcast on a television in the corner. People in China were getting ill from a new disease. We could see emergency vehicles on the streets. People in masks and white coats knocked on doors, residents were wheeled out on stretchers.

Lila raised her hands in surrender. 'Very well. I'll do it. But Meg, I don't understand why you're being so stubborn. Aren't philosophers supposed to be the voice of reason? And you're the one who got us into this detective business in the first place.'

An unfair accusation. But in a sense she was right.

CHAPTER 4

Meg

THREE MONTHS EARLIER I WAS IN A QUEUE AT THE TOWN HALL FOR A Persian music concert organised by one of my former philosophy students. Security had been tightened since the recent attack on a mosque in New Zealand.

My large bag contained a cushion, a book for the interval, reading glasses, another pair for watching the performers, my purse, tissues and other things that women tend to have on hand. The man in front, perhaps Iranian, was forced to empty his bag. A tablet, coins, phone, keys, water bottle, chocolate bar and a box of condoms spilled onto the table.

I had a hand on the cushion, ready to disgorge the contents of my bag, when the security man looked up wearily and waved me through. Relief at not being inconvenienced changed to indignation. Did they think I was incapable of committing a terrorist act?

As I waited for the concert to start, I realised the guard's treatment fitted a pattern. I thought of the times when café staff turned their backs and chatted to colleagues when I reached the head of the queue. Retailer's eyes often swept over me to a younger customer. At gatherings, people usually looked beyond me for someone else to greet. Or, if they did talk, they never seemed to hear what I said. I once accidentally wandered into a media conference with the Premier; the guard merely shrugged. Then there was the young man who walked into me because he was preoccupied with his phone. He didn't apologise.

Old people become invisible, especially older women. Even when we're noticed, we're usually regarded as inconsequential, harmless or a waste of time. Except for the Queen. I amused myself by thinking of expressions used to denigrate or patronise elderly women: crone, witch, spinster, old maid, chirpy old lady, woman of a certain age; and if she tried to look attractive she was "mutton dressed as lamb".

The concert started and I turned my attention to the performance. But in the interval I resumed my reflections on elderly invisibility.

Simone de Beauvoir's book on old age regarded the elderly as an oppressed social class with no hope of liberation. A sad situation. Who wants to be ignored or treated as irrelevant? Except when being invisible can serve your purposes. It occurred to me that a spy organisation or a group of assassins consisting of old women might have anadvantage. No one would pay attention to what they were doing. They could slip into forbidden territory, mingling anonymously in crowds. Security camera operators would zoom past them, never suspecting elderly women might be a danger. Why hadn't ASIO or the CIA thought of that?

My mind was filled with possibilities by the concert interval. I imagined recruiting a gang of old women to be undercover agents. What would they be called: the Grey Ghosts, the White Spectres, the Senior Sleuths or the Killer Crones? I decided that final name wouldn't be right. My gang would not commit murder; the Grey Ghosts would be a force for good.

Thoughts of the Grey Ghosts were pushed aside when I met Lila Gatti for a coffee in North Fitzroy the next morning. I'd met her recently at my book club. She had impressed me with her irrepressible ability to enjoy life. However, her mood was unusually sombre; her son had a fever.

'He'll recover. Dan's got a strong constitution.' She sighed. 'The doctors say his health is so good that he could have a normal lifespan. You understand that it's not *my* old age that I'm worried about.'

I didn't know what to say. John and I decided not to have children. Or rather he decided, and as usual, I agreed.

We sipped our coffee in silence, and then it occurred to me how to cheer up Lila. I told her about the Grey Ghosts. She was amused.

'You're partly wrong. I'm an old woman – but I'm not invisible.' She tugged at her purple polka-dotted harem pants. 'They don't want to see us. If I wore my purple turban, a scruffy caftan and put my lipstick on crooked, they would think I'm a dotty old woman about to preach about Jesus, or beg them for money. They might presume I'm going to do some cultural thing and make them feel guilty about white invasion. Or that I'm demented and will cause a scene.

'It's interesting how people, especially men, are embarrassed when an old woman does something strange. I think they fear contamination. I might touch them with my old lady hands, spray them with saliva or pollute them with my old lady smell. It's surprising what you can get away with when people are doing their best to avoid you and pretend you aren't doing what you're doing.

Lila was on a roll. 'There's a famous sociologist who used to break social rules – like eating a meal with his fingers at a restaurant – and observe how people reacted. Sometimes the diners would get angry. More often they pretended it didn't happen.'

I was amused, but also disconcerted. I couldn't imagine doing something like that.

She laughed at my reaction. 'What I really want to say is that your idea is brilliant. And it's not impossible to put it into practice. After I left the public service, I worked for a few organisations, including a detective agency. I have contacts. But what we need is someone with a good mind for logistics.'

I wanted to protest. I hadn't meant to be taken so seriously. Lila put up a hand to stop me. 'Wait. I have just the right person in mind.' She took out her phone.

That evening I was introduced to Dorothy Arden at the Gardener's Arms It had been a shaky start for the Grey Ghosts.

'Dorothy, this is Margaret.'

She'd stared at me with deep-set eyes. A large, broad nose made her more formidable. I tried informality.

'I'm Meg. Are you Dot?'-

She rose. 'Not a Dot, I'm a full-fledged Dor-o-thy.' On her feet she was a colossus. Her light grey wavy hair was clipped short. No earrings or jewellery. She was wearing jeans, sneakers and a close-fitting pullover. Dorothy was a few years younger than Lila, but in much better shape. This was a woman who worked out in a gym. I don't think she approved of me.

'How did you two meet?' I finally dared to ask when she had settled back into her seat.

Lila laughed. 'I walked into a pub one day and there was this old bat serving drinks behind the counter.'

'I didn't like having riff-raff in my pub,' countered Dorothy, 'and would have thrown her out if it hadn't looked like a job for a front-end loader. But since I couldn't get rid of her, and there was no one else around, I thought I might as well talk to her.'

'We found we were united in our hatred of platform shoes, radio shock jocks and the Melbourne Cup.'

Dorothy nodded. 'We're against animal cruelty.'

'And we had been fans of Daddy Cool, back in the day.'

'No, that was you. I preferred AC/DC.'

They were leaning towards each other, stifling giggles.

'All I was allowed to like,' I said, 'was classical music and some jazz.'

We all laughed, and Dorothy even smiled at me.

CHAPTER 5

Meg

THE COFFEE AND BISCUITS WERE FINISHED; DOROTHY CLOSED HER notebook. 'That's settled. We can tell Mr Todd our plan.' She turned to Lila. 'We'll say you were in a car accident. Not hurt, but shaken up. Your balance is shaky and you need one of those four wheeled walkers and hospice care to get over it. What do you think?'

Lila nodded. 'I won't have to disguise being slow on my feet. Let's hear what Mr Todd is offering to pay.'

Dorothy drove me home from the lawyer's office after the arrangements were made for Lila's stay. There was no conversation; Dorothy was cross. I wasn't acting according to her conception of how things should go. I was making life difficult for her friend Lila, and she didn't understand why.

Her silence made me nervous but I was glad she didn't question me. I had been in awe – and a little frightened – of Dorothy and her abrupt, uncompromising manner since my first visit to the Gardener's Arms. It was raining, traffic on the main road was heavy and the entrance to my *cul-de-sac* was blocked by a line of cars. 'Just let me off here.'

'You'll get wet.'

'No matter.' All I wanted was to get away from Dorothy's disapproval to the peace and comfort of my flat.

Dorothy stopped at the kerb. 'Have a think. You can always change your mind. Like you did last time.'

I grimaced. She was right. When Lila found a case for us to solve, I refused to have anything to do with it.

'I'm a philosopher,' I had told them. 'I live the life of the mind. I'm comfortable in my ivory tower.'

I was persuaded in the end because meeting Dorothy and Lila was the best thing that had happened to me for a long time. I was afraid that I would never see them again if I turned my back on their scheme.

But this plan was different. I was *not* going into a nursing home.

I grabbed my handbag, slammed the door and bolted through the rain to my flat.

CHAPTER 6

Meg

EVERYTHING WAS AS I LEFT IT. THE BOOK I HAD BEEN READING WAS ON the lounge room table. I could see another book beside the lamp through the open bedroom door. The rain stopped as I reached the stairs. A ray of sunshine had found the armchair that overlooked my neighbour's garden. I was home, but I didn't feel the relief I'd expected. I needed a change of clothes, a shower and a cup of tea.

I undressed in front of the bathroom mirror. I usually avoided looking at myself – lipstick can be applied without a close examination of my face – but I felt compelled to make a closer inspection.

I'm barely five foot tall, with a body turned scrawny, skin drooped beneath what had been a straight jawline. Wrinkles circled my neck, small breasts sagged over flesh that scarcely hid the skeleton underneath. Further down was an almost denuded bush of pubic hair. Below that were mottled, purple-veined hips.

I looked up quickly at bloodless lips, a nose that stuck out over a receding jaw: the face of a witch, a crone, an old woman. The rosy complexion that I inherited from my English ancestors had turned pallid. Bit by bit, year by year, I was turning into a ghost. The dimples that my friends admired had become cadaverous hollows. Gravity had pushed my mouth into a severe hangdog expression. When I first noticed the glum look that accompanied old age I tried to compensate with a tight smile. This was hard to hold; it looked like I had been given a facelift by an incompetent surgeon.

I put my hand up to caress the wispy white hair framing my face. Neatly styled but hardly thick enough to hide my scalp. My mother used to say that a woman should never neglect her appearance. I always followed that advice, though who cared anymore?

My mother. I had turned into a caricature of her. In my features I saw her face and detected disapproval of what I had become.

But I expected that from her. She never accepted my interest in philosophy, or my friends. She approved the marriage to John because he was a university professor, but she was furious when I divorced him. But I loved my career as a philosophy teacher, my friends were a continuing joy, and I never regretted my divorce.

So much for my mother's opinion. I stuck out my tongue at the reflection, then felt guilty.

'All I have is you,' she'd said as we sat in our garden the day after my father's funeral. Her voice had been soft, laden with sadness, deeply wounded by life's treatment.

I had taken her hand. 'That can't be right, Mother.' But I realised that that she had been right. She never liked living in Australia and didn't have any close friends. Charity work kept her busy but never interested her.

'And all you have is me,' she continued.

That wasn't true. I had school friends and was about to start a new life as a university student. She had stared into my face, daring me to disagree. It *was* true, I admitted to myself. None of my friends were all that close. I would rather sit home with a book than talk to people I didn't know in a pub or at a party.

She'd pressed my hand and drawn it towards her. 'I want you to have a good life. I want you to find friends worthy of your respect.'

I knew what she meant. She worried that the university was full of socialists, beatniks and hippies.

'I want you to be happy,' mother had said as she pressed my hand to her heart, as if dedicating herself to make that possible.

I already knew that our ideas of happiness were different. I resented her attempt to bind me to her. But with my hand on her heart, I couldn't suppress an upwelling of love, pity and gratitude. I wasn't going to sacrifice myself to please her, but I would do what I could to make the rest of her life better.

My lack of success was inevitable. I felt regret and guilt when I remembered how often I failed her – particularly in her final months when she begged me to get her out of the care home.

I stepped out of the shower and rubbed vigorously with a towel. The shared features with my mother reappeared in the mirror between swipes of the towel. Our physical similarities could not be denied, nor could our deeper character traits. We were what pop psychology called "introverts". We did not easily make friends. We dreaded large social gatherings. We sometimes went along with what others wanted because it was easier than raising objections.

But I wasn't afraid to tell people the truth, whatever they thought of me, I told myself as I put on my dressing gown. That was one of the things that being a philosopher had done for me.

I had no intention of reconsidering my refusal to take up residence at Sunnyvale when I sat down with a cup of tea. As I sipped, I couldn't help thinking that I needed to explain to myself why I was so strongly averse to being in a nursing home, even as a temporary resident. An unexamined life, so Socrates had said, is not worth living.

Some of this aversion, I decided, must come from childhood experiences. I had memories of our church choir singing carols every Christmas to the residents in a nursing home. The smell was the worst – a combination of urine and disinfectant. The residents were lined up in rows in the lounge room, some in wheelchairs, the rest sitting on shabby sofas or uncomfortable dining room chairs. We sang, but there was no sign from the residents that they enjoyed our singing or cared about our presence. They just sat there, sometimes coughing or fidgeting, but mostly unresponsive. I was always glad to leave.

I knew nursing homes were no longer that repulsive. The place where my mother lived didn't smell bad. Residents were encouraged to be active, although most struggled with mobility. All understood it would be their final home.

A negative reaction to being in a nursing home is understandable in those afraid of death. I don't share those thoughts. I have always agreed with Epicurus and Spinoza that death brings conscious existence to an end. Why fear a situation that you cannot experience?

I put down the empty cup and stared at the night through the lounge window.

I can't live like this. People sneak into my room and steal my things.

I doubted my mother.. She hid things away and then forgot where she put them. There had been an emotional experience when she tried to embroider her name on a shirt. The thread became tangled and she pricked her finger, spilling blood on the garment.

I reached out to help, but she pulled away and clutched it to her face. Tears fell on the cloth bunched in her hands.

I couldn't stop her tears as she leaned against me, repeatedly saying, 'I want ..'

I realised she wasn't concerned about her belongings. She was weeping because she had lost control over herself and her world. She wanted to go home and be the person she once was. I remembered my own tears; crying not just for her, but foreseeing the future that awaited me.

That was it, I thought as I took my empty cup to the kitchen. Losing control. Old age is an inevitable process of degeneration. It's downhill all the way. You not only lose your looks, as I already had. You lost your agility, your ability to experience passion and joy, and often you lost the things that were central to personal identity – your capacity to think, communicate, even to recognise the people you love. "Anna", my mother called me in the last months of her life. She had confused me with her sister.

A nursing home was where they put you when you lost your ability to be an active, rational being and became a body that needed to be managed.

I shuddered; I wanted nothing to do with nursing homes.

'Why dwell on the disabilities of old age?' Lila often admonished me for my old lady habits and pessimism about my future. 'I object to thinking of old age as a period of life that separates us from everyone who is actively living and enjoying their lives. People can suffer a disability at any age. You lose an ability to do one thing, so you do another.'

'Physical and mental degeneration are real,' I had pointed out.

'But why wait around for it to happen?'

I laughed at her. No amount of positive thinking was going to stave off the effects of ageing. But I couldn't help thinking that her view was the right one to take. Spinoza said that there was no point in thinking about death. Perhaps there was as little sense in dwelling on the infirmities of old age. My favourite philosophers, the Stoics, warned about living in fear of future calamities. Concentrate on life in the present, they said.

I prepared for bed. I thought I would have trouble sleeping, but I quickly dozed off and didn't wake until morning light was filtering through the curtains.

The rain had stopped and the sun had risen when I opened the door to my balcony. Fresh, clean air bathed my face. I breathed deeply and felt renewed.

I might end up as a drooling old women in a nursing home but I had my health, the ability to think – not all that much diminished – and to know when people were reasoning badly. I smiled when I remembered that Lila had called my philosopher skills my "superpowers".

I had my friends and things to do. I was ready to face new challenges. I completed my morning rituals of coffee, reading the news, brushing my teeth, dressing – and then I phoned Lila.

'I've changed my mind. I'll go into the nursing home. You can stay with Dan.'

Lila breathed deeply. 'Are you sure? I don't want you to think you have to do what you really don't want to do.' She paused. 'Don't mind Dorothy. She gets an idea of how she thinks things ought to happen and gets cross if we don't comply.'

'No, it's not Dorothy. I've had a think. You were right. I was being irrational. It's true I dislike the idea of being in a nursing home, but I'm not likely to be in danger of death or imprisonment.' I was able to laugh at the idea.

'If you're threatened by sadistic nurses or homicidal residents, all you'll have to do is get on your phone and we'll come to the rescue.'

'What will you do? Send in the army?' We laughed.

Lila caught her breath. 'I have to say I'm relieved. I could have continued to visit Dan, but it's much easier this way.'

'Dorothy was right. I'm the obvious person.'

'About Dorothy…' Lila was thinking. 'It's Sunday and Dorothy will be at her church. Afterwards she does some housework and phones her son in Seattle and her daughter in Berlin. Then she's free. Why don't we all meet at the Gardener's Arms for lunch? They have a good chicken parma. We can make our final arrangements. You should be able to take up residence at Sunnyvale early next week. The sooner the better, don't you agree?

Early next week? I wanted to protest. But Lila was right. Let's get this over with.

CHAPTER 7

Jenny

SHE IS IN A FOG. HER HEAD ACHES AND SHE FEELS NAUSEOUS. JENNY MOVES around to find a more comfortable position. There are of voices near her bed.

'Look, you can't say she's comfortable.'

'She's having a dream. Nothing to be concerned about.'

She opens her eyes, but their features are blurry and the effort makes her headache worse.

'She's awake but she can't even focus, she's so heavily drugged.' A man is speaking. 'Mother, say something.'

Her eyes close again. Jenny sees a small boy appear in the doorway of the garage wheeling his bicycle. He is angry. He tosses hair out of his eyes and clenches little fists. 'Mother, say something.'

Recognition. It's Colin, her son. Jenny wants to speak, but when she tries no words come.

'She can't even talk.'

'We must keep her on drugs for the protection of herself and others. She's had episodes of hysteria, running around screaming and hurling accusations at people.'

Jenny doesn't like that voice. She wishes she could put something over her ears to avoid hearing it.

'How could this happen? Less than a month ago she was downstairs, perfectly fine. She could communicate. She could remember things. And she certainly wasn't hysterical.'

'Sometimes dementia progresses rapidly, and changes of personality are a common result.' The voice is cool, matter-of-fact.

'Is she going to be like this from now on?'

'Your mother's much calmer up here. Her illness was made worse by her close association with Sara Brighouse. That woman encouraged her to develop the paranoid delusions that often accompany dementia. Now that we've taken her away from this bad influence I think we can expect some improvement in her condition.'

Sara.

Jenny wants to protest. She mouths words, still no sound.

'Can't you stop giving her drugs? She's not going to get better if you keep knocking her out.'

The cool voice becomes colder. 'I assure you, for the time being it's necessary. If you have questions, ask the doctor, or better yet, have a talk with her aunt. She knows what Jenny has been going through.'

'Her aunt!' Colin snorts. He is moving around, ready to leave. Jenny doesn't want him to go and reaches towards him. He takes her hand and holds it. She wants to speak to him about Sara, but the light dims. When she opens her eyes again her hand is empty and he is gone.

CHAPTER 8

Meg

Lila drove me to Sunnyvale in a van borrowed from her brother, a vehicle that smelled strongly of dog. I hoped my clothes wouldn't pick up the stench. We drove over the river into a belt of prosperity. Large residences sat behind stone walls or clipped hedges, capped with gabled roofs. We passed driveways that separated immaculate lawns and rows of cedars, in the distance were broad porches and vine-covered verandas. I caught the occasional glimpse of a rose garden and a patch of magnolias.

We crossed a main road and entered an estate built on the grounds of a former mental asylum. An old domed building loomed on the hill ahead of us. We saw a cluster of comfortable middle class houses before Lila steered into the drive beside a sign that announced our destination.

Sunnyvale Residential and Care Home: Residents and Visitors Only

We passed through an iron gate flanked by a high brick wall that surrounded the facility.

'Here we are.' Lila pulled into a parking place.

Too soon, I thought. Everything was happening quickly. I wanted to pause, get my bearings and brace myself for what lay ahead.

In front of us was a new rectangular two storey brick building.. A covered walkway led to the reception. Two narrow roads ran past the entrance – one to an underground carpark and the other to a barrier with a sign that said "Private". I could see that road ended at a single storey brick cottage.

I was disappointed to discover that Sunnyvale had no garden. There was only room for a few hardy succulents between the wall and the main building. Two young Japanese maples were trying to thrive in a shady plot near the reception entrance. Fortunately, across the road was a park with a small pond and a grove of trees. I was relieved to find an escape into nature at hand; walking in gardens or parks always helped me relax.

Lila was first out of the van. She put up a hand to stop me from moving.

'Wait, let me help you out.' She retrieved the walking frame that Dorothy had found in the back of the car and pushed it towards me. 'Remember, you're supposed to be feeble and shaky. Don't move without this thing. You've got to remember to always use it.'

We had settled on the idea that I had suffered a bad fall in my flat. I had escaped serious injury but my sense of balance and confidence were shaken and I needed to recover in a place where I would be looked after.

We were expected. The well-groomed, middle-aged woman behind the desk wore a name badge. Sylvie smiled, hesitated and then handed Lila the form to be filled out. I was annoyed, but told myself that incapacity was part of my disguise.

A month had been judged sufficient for my stay. I expected to be out much sooner. I wanted to meet Sara Brighouse to see if I could communicate with her and observe who she interacted with and how she was treated. The building was not large. The website said that it had space for 50 residents; it was a self-contained community where most people ate and socialised together. If someone or something was frightening Mrs Brighouse, it shouldn't be difficult to find the cause.

Sylvie collected the form from Lila and handed it to me. I signed it.

'You're fortunate,' she told me. 'The rooms are in demand. We had a short term vacancy because Mr Varney – he's the Hampstead mayor – took his mother on a cruise.'

I could see past the reception area into a large room where some residents were sitting. I heard a television but I was pleased to note that it was being ignored. One person was reading, another was paging through a magazine and two women were talking, leaning in towards each other's hearing aids.

'We pride ourselves on providing a comfortable, relaxed environment where residents can live at their own pace.' Sylvie was again talking directly to Lila. 'And we have a wide range of medical services, including physiotherapy and psychological counselling. We have our own hairdressing salon and a library. There's also a gymnasium in the basement.' She gave me a dubious look. 'I am sure she will have a pleasant stay with us. Some people who come for a temporary visit like it so much that they decide to become permanent residents.'

That couldn't possibly happen to me. This place was well beyond my means.

Sylvie bent down and spoke slowly, as if I was hard of hearing or slow to comprehend. 'Would you like a little tour now, or would you prefer to rest in your room?'

I said I was happy to take the tour. It would be a chance to check the place out. I could also regard myself as a visitor rather than a resident for a final few minutes.

Lila left my suitcase at the desk and Sylvie led us into the common room.

'Normally Miss Barr, the manager, would be here to welcome you and have a chat. She's busy with a visitor this afternoon. But I can tell you everything you need to know.'

I had to focus on guiding my walker over the carpet. The common room was large with a kitchenette in one corner and several rows of chairs in front of a small stage which held the television. Comfortable lounge chairs surrounded small tables at the back of the room. The woman reading a book looked up at me with interest and waved. I had no time to stop and introduce myself as Sylvie marched through a door on the other side. We paused at the entrance to the dining room. The wooden tables were covered with cheerful, checked tablecloths set for the next meal.

'Dinner is at six. But if she prefers she can eat in her room.'

Off to the side was a smaller and gloomier lounge. Each corner held large dark leather armchairs that would swallow a small person like me. . They would be good for private conversations with Lila.

Back in the common room I noticed the television had been switched to a news channel. It showed pictures of the Chinese city where residents had been forced indoors to escape infection by the new disease. The empty streets looked strange and forbidding, like something out of a surrealist painting.

We took the lift to the basement, and Sylvie pointed to the store room where I could put anything superfluous to life at Sunnyvale. 'It's always locked,' she said. 'The key is at the reception.'

We poked our heads into the small gym that she didn't expect me to use. It was empty. Then we returned to inspect the resident accommodation on the ground floor. Some rooms had resident names. The dormitory atmosphere was relieved by a series of alcoves along the corridor where people could sit, chat or look at the driveway if they got tired of being in their rooms. I caught a glimpse of pictures in the spaces between the doors: landscapes, old photographs, perhaps of local historic sites. At the end of the corridor was the original portrait of Josephine Wakefield that featured on the back of the Sunnyvale brochure.

'She's kind of our patron saint,' said Sylvie. 'She lives here but she mostly stays in her residence. Sometimes she pays us a visit and you may have the opportunity of meeting her.' She made this sound like a sought-after privilege. I presumed that the cottage with the private road belonged to her.

'Her foundation has big plans for Sunnyvale. She is going to use her fortune to establish the Josephine Wakefield Centre for Geriatric Research. It will be a world class facility with a residence and hospital for senior citizens.'

Resident guinea pigs, I thought.

We stopped at a bedroom near the end of the corridor. The door was ajar.

'We don't lock the doors for safety reasons,' said Sylvie. 'But our security is tight. We monitor everyone who comes in and out.' Sylvie addressed Lila. 'She can lock her valuables in the safe at the reception if she wants. But we don't have serious problems with theft.'

She held the door open. I braced myself, took a deep breath and stepped over the threshold. My first feeling was relief. The room was nothing like the one where they'd put my mother. It did not look or feel like a hospital ward. It was more like a hotel that prided itself on making guests feel cosy. It was larger than I'd expected and the bed, bigger than a normal single, was covered with a cheerful blue and white checked doona. Beside it was a comfortable looking chair for visitors and a wooden table with drawers. The carpet was thick and grey, the curtains off white. Two chairs and a coffee table were positioned to provide a view out the window. The effect was neat, tasteful and impersonal. You were expected to make it into your home by adding your pictures and knick-knacks.

I pushed my walker to the window and looked at a courtyard bordered by raised garden beds that almost reached the bottom of the windows. Cast iron garden chairs, a table and a stone birdbath sat beneath a canopy. The space was empty. Where did the residents spend most of their day? Did they isolate themselves in their rooms, coming together only for meals? I was beginning to feel apprehensive. How was I going to find out anything if they turned out to be reclusive?

Sylvie directed us to the bathroom and pointed out the safety features to Lila. I was given an exaggerated smile of reassurance. 'I'm sure you will feel safe and comfortable but you, can always let us know if you want anything or need help. All you have to do is pick up a phone. There's one in here and one beside your bed.' She indicated the red handset near the toilet and pointed in the direction of the bedroom. She looked at her watch. 'Judy will be here in a moment with your case. She can help you get settled.'

Lila and I embraced before I waved goodbye with a feeling of abandonment that I tried to repress.

CHAPTER 9

Meg

THE NEXT MOMENT A PRETTY, RED-HAIRED YOUNG WOMAN IN A BLUE uniform breezed in. The name tag "Judy" was pinned on her blouse.

'Here's your things. Do you want me to help you unpack?' She spoke in the chirpy voice that people often used when they are addressing the very old or the very young.

I declined her help and she turned to leave.

'Wait,' I said. 'Do you know Mrs Brighouse? Do you know where her room is?'

I realised that I was asking a question that an employee might find over-inquisitive for a new arrival. But Judy was merely surprised.

'Do you know her?'

'She's a friend of someone I know.'

Judy grinned. 'She's living very close to you.' She pointed at the wall next to my bed. 'She's in there most of the time, but she keeps herself to herself.' Then she waved goodbye and dashed away.

How convenient to be housed beside the woman I was supposed to be watching. I opened my door and saw a chair in the alcove opposite. I could sit there with a book and keep track of her visitors. I would be on the spot if anything happened to frighten her.

I shut my door and unpacked. I had decided that my best clothes would be required. Sunnyvale was not the place to wear jeans or sweat pants to the dining room. I brought the good suit that I wore at formal occasions and a few nice dresses. They were out of fashion but surely that wouldn't matter. There were also combinations of slacks and blouses. My pumps were old but they would have to do. I took out several books, and put the largest one on the bedside table. I was sure it would be more than adequate for my temporary stay at Sunnyvale.

In the corner of my case was a small packet of Earl Grey tea. I peeked into the cupboard beneath the sink near the bed. Yes, there was a kettle and a few cups and saucers. Whatever happened at Sunnyvale, I would be able to make myself a decent cup of tea. Then it occurred to me that could be the access to Mrs Brighouse. I could knock on her door, introduce myself and offer her a cup of my tea. We could have a conversation and perhaps the whole case could be wrapped up before the end of the afternoon.

I looked out the door and found the corridor empty. I walked to Mrs Brighouse's door and knocked softly. No answer. I tried again, listened, but no sound came from her room.

Judy said she didn't mingle. I didn't want to disturb or frighten her. Perhaps it would be better to approach her in a social setting – in the dining room or the common room.

I turned back to my room and stopped by the window to watch a middle-aged couple walking towards the building with a bag and bottle of wine. Someone visiting a relative, I thought.

I was startled as my shoulder was prodded.

I turned to face a wild-haired woman who had used her cane to get my attention. She shuffled closer, baggy trousers barely clung to her hips and bunched at her ankles. A sloppy pullover stretched over her hunched back.

She looked angry, and I backed away. 'Who are you?'

She shook her head and pointed at Mrs Brighouse's door. 'That room is supposed to be mine.' She planted herself in front of me, feet apart, and thumped her cane on the floor. 'They promised me that room and then they gave it to her.' Spittle was collecting at the side of her mouth.

She looked like a rabid animal and I stepped back towards the safety of my room. She followed me.

'You tell her from me she should get out. That room is mine.'

To my relief she then lurched away.

Back in my room — and breathing normally — I considered that the answer to the mystery might have revealed herself. The wild, unkempt woman wanted Mrs Brighouse's room; she was probably harassing her at every opportunity. Our client said that his mother was timid; being threatened by a woman with a cane would be enough to frighten an elderly resident.

I was pleased. All I needed was to get Mrs Brighouse to confirm she had been threatened by the mad woman. I didn't think it would be difficult to find witnesses.

I looked forward to talking to Lila. I was almost ready to announce that our mission had been accomplished.

CHAPTER 10

Jenny

A DIM LIGHT IS FILTERING THROUGH THE BLINDS. SHE HAS BEEN DREAMING about her mother. She closes her eyes again and the memories return.

They are sitting together on the couch in the lounge room of her mother's flat in Hampstead. Sunlight comes in from the large bay window and spills over the blue carpet. The mantelpiece above the fireplace is heaped with pictures, vases, figurines and other souvenirs of her mother's life. In a darker corner is the grand piano, delivered a few weeks ago by three men who heaved it up the stairs and manoeuvred it sideways to get it through the door.

'It's for Leo,' her mother had explained. 'He needs it for his work.'

Leo's work, Jenny knows, is playing a piano at a jazz club in the city. Her mother had taken her one night. Leo and three men played their instruments in a cramped downstairs room that smelled of cigarettes and liquor. People listened on wooden chairs, jerking up and down to the beats, tapping their feet and sometimes clapping. During the day, Leo sat by the piano, a cigarette always in hand, making marks on a piece of paper. 'Composing songs,' her mother said and gave him an affectionate tap on the shoulder.

Her mother's face is so close to hers that Jenny has trouble making out her features apart from the clear grey eyes. Her mother's mouth brushes her ear, and wavy brown hair caresses her cheek. Her body smells of roses.

'My dear little Jen.' She laughs and kisses her forehead. 'We will have such an adventure together. A new life for us.'

She feels warm and comfortable in her mother's arms. 'I love you,' she says. She would like nothing better than to stay on that couch alongside her mother all day; for every day.

She squeezes her mother's arm. They enjoy the tranquillity until she hears noises in the next room. A door opens and shuts, footsteps approach, becoming louder. Leo appears in their room and their peaceful time is over. Her mother starts to rise. Jenny doesn't want her to leave and clings tightly to her arm.

'Enough, Jen,' her mother says, pushing her off.

Leo is angry. 'You bitch. You're cheating on me. Don't deny it. They're talking about you and Douglas at the Club.'

Her mother indicates that Jenny should leave the room but she leaves the door ajar and waits behind it. If Leo tries to hurt her mother, she'll scream and Rosie or Suzie will come.

'And Douglas is not the only one,' continues Leo. 'There's that bloke from London. You were seen having dinner with him.'

Her mother's laugh tinkles like the keys on the piano. 'What? Do you have spies following me?'

'What else have you got to hide? You don't know what it is to be faithful. You and your friends.' He screeches. 'Sometimes I think I could kill you.' Jenny holds her breath. This is not the first time Leo has said those awful words.

Her mother reacts calmly. 'Don't be ridiculous. I'm not cheating on you. Can't I have friends? Can't I go out and have a social life while you're playing a piano in that wretched bar?'

There's a long silence. From the half open door, Jenny can see that her mother has moved closer to him and is about to put her hand on his shoulder.

'After we're married you won't have to play in those low dives and we can be together all the time, if that's what you want.'

'Is your brother bothering you about your inheritance? Has he been threatening you?'

My mother's tinkling laugh cuts him short. 'Is that what you're really worried about – my money?'

'Dearest, Lizzie, please. I'm worried that they're pestering you. Your brother and his social climbing wife.'

Jenny can tell that he is about to take her mother in his arms. This is how it always ends: words of love and sloppy kisses.

She hurries away. She doesn't like Leo. She doesn't want him to take her mother away to London. She knows that he doesn't like her either. He took her to the zoo once and she could tell he hated having to endure the company of a child. He was only doing it to please her mother, and that was the way it would always be in London.

I am the baggage he must put up with if he wants to be with mother.

She sees Rosie coming to fetch her. '

'I've been looking for you. Lunch is ready.' Rosie takes her by the hand and squeezes it. 'Come now. Don't worry about their silly games.'

'Yes Rosie.' She follows.

It's Sunday afternoon, and Jenny and Rosie are alone in her mother's flat.

'Let's play the tickling game,' Rosie says. She takes Jenny by the arm and they go upstairs where Rosie has a new yellow blanket on her bed. 'Do you like it?'

Rosie removes her blouse and skirt, then Jenny takes off her own clothes, and they lie together on the bed.

"I know where you are ticklish,' Rosie brushes her fingers lightly down Jenny's shoulders and back.

In response, she giggles and squirms. 'Stop,' she implores. But Rosie doesn't. Her tickles become caresses and she moves her hand at first along Jenny's thigh and then strokes the soft flesh between her legs.

'Touch me there,' Rosie says and takes Jenny's hand, directing it to soft, moist flesh.

Jenny does what Rosie asks and feels Rosie pushing against her, harder and harder.

"Do you like it?' Rosie asks. But Jenny doesn't know whether the feeling she gets is good or bad. It's strange and disturbing, not exactly pleasant, but she doesn't pull away. When Rosie finishes they cuddle in the sweaty sheets. Jenny feels safe and comfortable in Rosie's bed.

'Will you come and sleep in my bed tonight?' Jenny asks Rosie. 'If my mother doesn't come?' She knows that her mother will be with Leo at the Club.

'Yes, when your mother goes out.'

'Rosie.' Jenny's lips say her name but the sound doesn't come.

'Wake up, Mrs Mueller, your breakfast is here.' Nancy opens the blinds and Jenny sees that it's late morning.

'Something special today. A nice omelette.'

Jenny looks at the yellow cylinder on her plate and shakes her head.

'Come now. If you eat up I'll take you for a walk.'

When Jenny finishes breakfast, Nancy finds her slippers and helps her stand. Once on her feet she wants to walk by herself but Nancy insists on taking her arm. They move slowly into the corridor, steer around a trolley full of dirty plates and along a passageway with rooms on one side. Some doors are open; people are watching television or dozing in their beds. They come to a corner and they hear noises from the next corridor. Someone is shouting. Nancy guides her to a chair.

'Stay here, Mrs Mueller. I'll be back in a tick.' Then she is gone.

Jenny sits and looks around. The corridor is wide and there's a door at the far end. She rises and heads towards it. As she approaches, her sense of urgency increases. She needs to get out and do something, but what? Then she remembers that she needs to talk to Sara. She must go downstairs and find Sara.

She reaches the door and turns the handle. It's locked. She jerks at it in vain, crying in frustration. Nancy calls out. Jenny looks around and behind the nurse is Harry, rapidly approaching with his syringe.

CHAPTER 11

Meg

I WOULD HAVE PREFERRED DINNER IN MY ROOM, WITH TIME TO THINK ABOUT my impressions of Sunnyvale and to prepare myself for meeting its residents. But I want to get the job done as quickly as possible; dinner was a chance to learn more about life at the care home and Sara Brighouse. I had studied the picture provided by her son. I'm not good at recognising faces but hers was distinctive: high cheek bones and forehead, deeply set blue eyes and straight reddish hair framing a narrow face. If I arrived at the dining room early, I would be able to identify her and perhaps have a chance to talk.

I put the picture aside and studied my clothes in the wardrobe. I wanted to make a good impression but I also wanted something unobtrusive. Remembering what Lila had said about the advantages of being able to fade into the background, I took out my grey skirt and light blue silk blouse.

My plan to arrive early was thwarted. A crowd of people had been waiting for the dining room door to open. They were moving inside to find their seats as I arrived.

Dinner was probably the event of the day for many of these people.

It didn't take long to recognise Sara Brighouse. She was sitting at a middle table dressed in pink, looking straight ahead, her body stiffly upright as if she were anticipating a formal occasion.

I sat opposite. Her eyes focused on me with surprise.

'I'm Meg,' I hoped my tone was reassuring. 'I'm new here.'

Her alarm increased and I became aware that a group had gathered behind me.

'Excuse me.' The voice was imperious and I turned to face a body enveloped in an enormous red tent. She was standing so close I had to twist and crane my neck to see her properly. I noticed a string of pearls that looked genuine, then a powdered neck, a frown, glaring eyes and a heap of hair piled on the top of her head. A few paces away, a tall, stooped woman leaning on her cane looked slightly apologetic. Next to her were three more well-dressed women waiting to take their places.

'This is our table and I have to inform you that you're sitting in my chair.'

'I'm sorry. I'm new here. I wasn't aware that seats are reserved.'

'This is our table. It's always been our table.' She was a school prefect laying down the unwritten rules of behaviour to the new girl. But I had a good reason for being where I was and I was not inclined to move.

The waitress rushed up. 'Please, Mrs Thorne, there's a place for you right over there.' She pointed at a table now occupied by a morose gentleman. I realised that my ability to get along in this place depended on a tactical retreat. I stood and, without looking up or apologising to the woman in pearls, moved towards the designated place.

'Thank you very much.' Her voice made it clear that she thought me ill-mannered.

My designated table was clearly not popular. I'm sure the glum expression on my dinner companion's face put them off.

'Hello. I'm Meg. I'm new here.'

He looked at me for a moment, nodded, and then looked away. It didn't appear that he was deliberately shunning me. It felt like his mind was occupied with other matters, as if it had no room left to consider the comings and goings of people around him.

'You won't get anything out of him.' The woman who sat down next to me smiled and introduced herself: 'Georgia, and here comes Wanda.'

Georgia was plump, well dressed in a brightly coloured, loose-fitting silk gown. Brown curls surrounded a round, friendly face. She smelled of rosewater.

Wanda was taller with blue rinse hair; a style that I thought had gone out of fashion. Other women and another man eventually found their way to our table and the meal was served. The food was superb and there was a plenty of it: a big piece of steak with lots of mash.

As I was eating, I glanced at the table I had been forced to abandon. I noticed that Sara Brighouse didn't talk to her companions. Her posture remained stiff and unyielding. She left most of her food. Unlike Sara, I couldn't break my mother's rule about eating everything on your plate. I was overfull by the end of the meal.

CHAPTER 12

Meg

GEORGIA INVITED ME FOR A HOT DRINK IN THE COMMON ROOM AFTER dinner. As we made our way to the counter in front of the kitchenette, we were greeted with a beatific smile from a tiny white-haired woman in an armchair.

'Welcome. I am glad you could come. I hope you have an enjoyable evening.'

I returned the greeting. She looked at me with a pleasant but absent expression.

'That's Hermione. She's sits here and greets everyone as if she's welcoming them to one of the soirees she used to give in her grand house in Hampstead. She's a good friend of Mrs Wakefield. We call her "the Angel of Sunnyvale".'

I got a cup of hot water and a bag of inferior tea from a lady behind the counter – disappointing for an establishment that prided itself on good service. 'The coffee's not good either,' Wanda warned me. 'There's a café around the corner where some of us go for a good morning cuppa.'

Georgia and Wanda guided me to a comfortable spot in the corner where we had a good view of residents coming and going.

'I'm an artist. Of sorts,' Georgia told me with a self-deprecating laugh. She had taught art in a school and now painted water colour landscapes, sometimes setting up her easel in the park next door. 'I have so many paintings in my room and my children won't take any more. Perhaps you would like one or two for your room.'

She launched into a description of the European exhibitions and galleries she had visited with her husband. He had been a company executive and an artist in his spare time.

Wanda's hobby was writing books for her grandchildren. 'Georgia illustrates them.'

Raised voices came from another corner of the room. Two bald, well-padded men in suits and drinking brandies were arguing. 'Decimate does not mean killing everyone. Just one in ten.'

The taller man waved off the definition. 'The Oxford dictionary allows it to mean "destroying a large number." Don't be such a purist.'

The first man was disdainful. 'I suppose it also allows "momentarily" to mean "soon" and "refute" to mean "deny".'

I sympathised. I am not a semantic purist but as a philosopher I abhor the way that "begs the question" has come to mean "raises the question".

Georgia laughed. 'Those two are retired public servants. They're our representatives on the board that runs Sunnyvale. The brandies are probably perks. They're always together and they rarely talk to anyone else. We think they're…you know?'

'Gay?' I offered.

She nodded.

'Who are those women over there?' I pointed to the group who ousted me from Sara Brighouse's table.

'We call them the Coterie. Most have been friends all their lives. They regard themselves as the elite. You know, there was always a group like that at every school.'

I didn't really know. Mine had emphasised academic achievement and required us to wear uniforms.

'Their leader is Mrs Chapman, that fat lady in pearls with her nose in the air. She has a bad word for everyone. The tall thin one with the cane is her lieutenant. She has the job of apologising for the mean things that her friend says. She'll apologise to you.'

'How about the lady in pink?' I indicated my neighbour who was sitting at the edge of the Coterie but not following in the conversation.

'That's Sara Brighouse. The Coterie adopted her because her family has money and she went to the same schools. She's a well-mannered lady. Not like them. But she's been upset since her best friend Jenny was moved. Sara's not been the same since and I think it won't be long before she's taken upstairs herself.'

'Upstairs?'

'That's where they put those in advanced stages of senility. They're locked in so there's no danger of them wandering around and getting into trouble.'

Or troubling the other residents, I thought.

'Some people down here are pretty far gone, as well. Hermione is an example. You might have noticed that the front door is locked. You can't get out without knowing the code. The ones who don't know it, or can't use it, are stuck inside. It's to stop them escaping onto the streets. But they'll give you the code. Just ask at the desk.'

I decided to get the door code as soon as possible and to commit it to memory.

Georgia pointed to a man sitting in the corner. 'His name is James Melling. He's a nice bloke, but he's dying of cancer. There's a hospital ward upstairs that provides palliative care.'

Melling was sitting on the edge of his chair and looked like he was in pain. He had the frame of a former athlete. He would have been tall and broad shouldered in his prime; the illness made him stooped and skeletal. His face was blueish grey and his eyes had sunk into cavities under the bony ridge of his forehead.

Poor man.

'How about the gloomy man who was sitting opposite me at dinner? The one who disappeared as soon as he had eaten.'

'That's Miles Reading. He's a sad case. He fell asleep while driving. His wife and two of their grandchildren were killed when the car crashed and rolled. He wasn't seriously hurt but he had a mental breakdown and that's why he came here. I've never seen any of his family visit. I think they've broken contact – or maybe he doesn't want them to come.'

'That's too bad,' My eyes were turned to the doorway. I hadn't seen the woman with the cane at dinner and was curious if she would be in the common room.

'I'm watching out for a woman who poked me with a cane this

afternoon,' I explained to Georgia and Wanda. 'An angry woman in baggy clothes.'

'Melanie!' said Georgia and Wanda together.

'Don't worry about her,' continued Georgia. 'Her bark is worse than her bite. She's always angry about something. Last week she was complaining that Judy, the little red-haired girl who runs errands, was stealing her mail. Best to ignore her when she's ranting.'

'You wouldn't believe from the way she dresses that Melanie comes from one of the best families in Melbourne,' added Wanda.

I wanted to ask whether they had seen Melanie confront Sara, but our conversation was interrupted by a sudden commotion.

CHAPTER 13

Meg

THE TWO RETIRED PUBLIC SERVANTS STOOD TO ATTENTION AS A TALL WOMAN entered. A cane tapped. An indication of her regal progress than any sign of infirmity. A squat woman with clipped hair and a haughty expression accompanied her. The manager, I presumed.

'Mrs Wakefield!' exclaimed Georgia.

Sunnyvale's matriarch proceeded to a chair prepared by one of the men, sat and arranged her shawl to cover her upper arms. The other board member brought her a glass of sherry. His offering looked like a form of obeisance. I looked back at Hermione; she stared reverently at Mrs Wakefield.

'She doesn't usually leave her residence. Do you want to introduce yourself?' Georgia's tone suggested that I might prefer not to. But I was curious to meet the woman who had played an important role in Melbourne social scene for generations.

I walked to the chair where she was flanked by the two courtiers and the matron who looked more like a bodyguard.

'I'm Margaret Thorne, a new arrival and I'm very pleased to meet you, Mrs Wakefield.' It felt like a curtsey would be in order.

She was a handsome woman who did not look her age. Her nose was large and her features were well-defined which added to her commanding presence. She was dressed in a long skirt and a pleated blouse, old fashioned but entirely suited to the dignified grandeur she conveyed in every gesture and movement. Her grey hair was elaborately styled, most likely done by the resident hairdresser.

Mrs Wakefield gave me a brief smile. 'I hope you will be comfortable here.'

It was a polite response, but I could see that she wasn't interested in talking to me. Her eyes shifted to someone who had come up beside me. It was the pearl necklace from dinner. I felt that she wanted to push me out of her way.

'Good evening, Vera,' said Mrs Wakefield. 'I'm so pleased you could be with us.'

I turned away as Vera Chapman simpered. The stocky woman had been assessing me.

'Mrs Thorne,' she said. 'You're the new arrival.'

I nodded.

'I'm Deidre Barr, the manager of Sunnyvale. I understand you've had a little accident and need time to recuperate. I hope you find your stay healing in every way.' There was a flicker of a smile. 'We should have a chat. Come to my office after breakfast tomorrow. 'It was a summons, not an invitation. I retreated to Georgia and Wanda. How did you like Mrs Wakefield?' asked Georgia.

'She's a snob, there's no denying it,' Wanda said, 'but after all, she belongs to what Melbourne regards as its upper crust.'

I thought I wouldn't mind if I never encountered her again.

Georgia pointed to the manager. 'Miss Barr is the one who runs the place. She's efficient but you don't want to get on the wrong side of her.'

'She wants to see me tomorrow, first thing.'

'To give you a list of rules,' said Wanda. 'It's like getting a talk from the headmistress. We all went through it.' She laughed and poured herself another cup of tea.

We were joined by three women, one almost as diminutive as me. They were university educated, one the wife of a barrister and the other two enjoyed professional careers. They were pleased to discover that I had been a university lecturer and a professor's wife. The sorting had been done and I was accepted as a member of their group.

'We go out for a coffee most mornings at 10.30,' said Georgia. 'You must join us.'

A man I hadn't noticed before approached our group. He was too young for an institution like Sunnyvale with wavy dark hair above a craggy face and an athletic build.

'Hello, ladies, what are your pretty heads gossiping about this evening?' He turned to me. 'I see the Queen Bee has given you her gracious royal greeting. Too bad Miss Piggy with the pearls is being so mean to you.'

'I've met worse.'

'Good girl.'

My face became hot with the effort of supressing my anger.

'A terrible man," said Georgia when he left. 'His name is Simon Long. I think he has a wasting disease. That's why he's here.'

As I was leaving, Vera Chapman's friend intercepted me at the door.

'I'm Catherine,' she said. 'I'm sorry about that misunderstanding over the seating. We're creatures of habit, and how were you to know? Please don't pay too much attention to Vera when she's like that. She's not a mean person. You'll find out that she can be generous and kind.'

She paused as if preparing to say something further, but her friend was waiting impatiently half way down the corridor.

I managed to say something appeasing, wished them both a good night and went to my room, but not before picking up the code to the front door from reception.

CHAPTER 14

Jenny

IT'S DARK WHEN SHE WAKES, CONFUSED ABOUT HER LOCATION. SHE WHIMPERS but is too frightened to cry out. She takes deep breaths to calm herself. Understanding comes.

I am Jennifer Mueller. I am in my room at Sunnyvale.

Her eyes turn to the wall seen by the dim light over the bathroom door. Dark cracks on its surface merge to form a bulge that looks like a weapon – a club or a gun. She shudders and closes her eyes.

She is in her mother's lounge, reclining with a book on the chair in the alcove. This is her private space. When she draws the curtains, no one knows she is there. She can ignore the lady who cleans the room, the visitors who come to see her mother, and even Leo when he is playing the piano.

The door opens suddenly and two people enter. She can tell one is her mother by sound of the heels on the floor.

'You're going to ruin me.' It's her uncle. 'I've worked for years to build up the business and now, thanks to you and your silly schemes, it's all going to go down the drain.'

Her mother pauses near the piano. 'You're being ridiculous. The business will be fine. Anyway, half of it belongs to me. We inherited it together, yet all these years you've collected most of the profits. I'm not taking them away from you, Robert.'

Uncle Robert sputters. Jenny does not want to peek through the curtains but she can picture the balding, portly uncle's face growing red while trying to control his temper.

'I've worked hard for both of us, and now you do this. And I should tell you that conditions haven't been good for business lately. There are lots of calls on our capital, and I'm married now and have the expense of setting up a household. Losing a lot of money at this time is unsupportable.' He's breathing heavily and makes a circuit of the room, brushing the curtain that conceals Jenny. She cowers, waiting for the storm.

Her mother remains calm. 'I'm marrying too. We have plans, and we also need money.'

Her uncle snorts. 'Plans! A jazz club in London! Can't you see that you'll be throwing our money away?'

Her mother plays a few notes with one finger on the piano. She is speaks softly but the words come out clipped and accusatory. 'You think that Leo and I are nothing but parasites.'

'What do you expect? A parasite is the right word for what you've been all your life. You travel, party and expect me to work hard to support you. And Leo is no different. What has he done with his life? He plays a piano at a jazz club and earns barely enough money for his drinks.'

The storm is here. Jenny wants to run to the kitchen, find Rosie. But she doesn't dare move or make a sound. Her book drops from her hand and she huddles against the back of the chair.

Her mother raises her voice. 'You expect *me* to be ashamed. Look at yourself, you misery guts. You wallow in self-pity. You want everyone to know how hard you're working, to feel sorry for you and to blame me for your pitiful life. And now you've married that grasping, social-climbing bitch, Josephine. She'll make your life hell. But you can't blame me for that.' She brings her fingers down hard on discordant notes.

'Stop it! I know you don't like Josephine, but you're going too far.'

Her mother becomes conciliatory. 'I'm sorry. To each his own. But you have no right to be critical of my choices.'

Uncle Robert stops pacing. Jenny can see them as dark shapes through the curtain. 'How can I help it when I see that you're about to ruin your life? And you have a child. Can't you see that all this wastrel

Leo wants is your money? When he's spent it all on his foolish schemes, he'll leave you. You're no spring chicken and he's not the fatherly type.'

There's a slap. Both are silent and Jenny holds her breath.

'I'm sorry,' says her uncle. 'We don't have to quarrel. I know you and Leo need more money. We can look at the books together and work out what the business can afford.'

'The money is mine. You can't deny it.'

Her uncle sighs. 'We'll talk again.'

'I don't see the point.'

The lounge door closes and Jenny realises he's gone. Her mother plays a few more notes on the piano and then leaves.

She hears a trolley approaching. The door to her room opens.

'Breakfast is here,' says Nancy.

CHAPTER 15

Meg

I THOUGHT ABOUT THE EVENTS OF THE DAY BEFORE OVER A CUP OF TEA. I had slept well, confident that I had found the reason for Sara Brighouse's fear. Melanie's rantings might be considered harmless by other residents, but I had the impression that it would not take much to frighten Sara. All I needed was a chance to talk to her and confirm my suspicions. I could use my interview with Deidre Barr to get more information. Perhaps Melanie was known for attacking people. Had she become a problem for the manager?

Judy knocked before I had finished dressing for breakfast. 'How are we this morning, Mrs Thorne?'

'We're well. But we could use a box of tissues. Could we bring them sometime this morning?'

My reply puzzled her, but she soon nodded, smiled and dashed away. I knew what she was thinking: old people say the strangest things.

I saw a familiar face on the way back to my room after breakfast. Professor Roderick Knight was a famous psychologist and had been one of my ex-husband's friends. We had sometimes invited him and his wife over for a meal. He shuffled, bent over a walker, apparently not noticing me. I intercepted him.

'Hello Rod, remember me? I'm Meg, John Thorne's first wife.'

He scrutinised me carefully and then apologised. 'Yes, of course.

Good to see you again, Meg. I haven't forgotten, it's just that I'm going blind. The trials of old age.'

He had been one of the pioneers of cognitive science. 'Are you still doing research?'

'Oh no. That's in the past and not just because I've lost most of my sight. I have a machine that magnifies print so I can read and I listen to talking books. Otherwise, I eat and sleep and do a bit of work in the garden. That's my life now.'

'There's a garden?'

'Yes, the window boxes in the courtyard. A gardener is supposed to come once a fortnight and someone does the watering. That's not enough to keep the weeds down. I potter around mostly in the morning. I can still distinguish a weed from a plant. A poor substitute for the large garden we had in the Dandenongs, but well, I've come to this...'

He shuffled away. 'Say hello to John from me.'

I don't think he remembered that John and I had parted many years ago.

It was too early for the meeting with the manager, so I prepared another cup of tea and sat near the window into the courtyard where Rod weeded. John. I hadn't thought about my married life for a long time. Not that my memories of our relationship were painful. Some, like our first encounter, were pleasurable.

'You have a very sharp mind. I like the way you defended Plato's view about universals in our tutorial.'

I looked up from my café seat. Standing behind me was the classical philosophy professor. He was my favourite teacher: clever, attractive. 'Do you mind if I join you. We can talk some more about Plato's views.

That's how it began. We met regularly for coffee to discuss philosophy – and then about the life we were going to have together once he got his divorce. I was in love for the first time. His attention and respect for my views made me feel like I had received the highest honour that the world could bestow.

John warned me that he had important work to complete. It was a series of books that would revolutionise the study of the relation between modern and ancient philosophy. He said his wife didn't understand.

I did.

John didn't want to be burdened with children. I had always assumed when growing up that I would be a mother. But I was willing to make sacrifices for his sake and the work that was important for him. I learned that he considered he was a much better thinker than me and that we would always be related as teacher to student.

We married shortly after I graduated. The teacher-pupil relationship didn't last. I embarked on my own independent work as a post-graduate student and was not inclined to defer to him or to believe in the great value of his project. I didn't always disguise my scepticism. When he announced seven years later that he was leaving me for another woman – a student in one of his classes – I wasn't surprised nor greatly upset. I had my own career as a philosopher and a lecturer's job in a university.

'I regret nothing,' I tell my friends when they try to sympathise with me as a betrayed wife. 'Not for falling in love. Not for my marriage nor my divorce.' In fact, my relationship with John taught me a lot and I will always be grateful to him for that.

He lives In Sydney with his wife and two children. We send each other cards at Christmas.

I looked at my watch. I was going to be late for my appointment. I moved as quickly as the walker would allow to reception where Sylvie pointed the way to her office.

Deidre Barr was waiting behind her desk. Everything in the room orderly. Papers needing attention were lined up in front of her, letters lay in a wire basket ready to be taken away. She motioned me to sit.

"I want to officially welcome you to Sunnyvale. Your stay will be short, but I hope pleasant.' She handed a sheet of paper to me.

'Our little community is peaceful and trouble free,' she said. 'But there are a few rules that all of us must observe. To those of us accustomed to a civilised society, these rules are simply a matter of common sense.' She looked at me sharply. Was she questioning whether I could be counted in the company of civilised people?

I glanced at the list. I was not supposed to make loud noises in my room after 9 at night or to hold parties in public spaces without permission. I nodded, folded the paper and put it in my handbag.

'Is there anything you would like to ask me?'

I folded my hands and straightened my back. 'Yes, as a matter of fact. I want to tell you that I was attacked by another resident yesterday afternoon.'

'Attacked? Were you hurt? Do you want to make a complaint?'

'No. I wasn't hurt – it wasn't much more than a prod with a walking stick.'

'Melanie!' The manager seemed relieved. 'She's harmless. I wouldn't worry about Melanie.'

'Just the same, she's an angry person. She's annoyed with my neighbour, Sara Brighouse. I'm worried she might be bothering her.'

Mrs Barr raised a hand to stop me talking and leaned forward. 'Mrs Thorne. I think we need to get a few things straight.' The tone wasn't reassuring.

'You were a teacher, and I suppose that you had a legitimate concern about the way people behaved in your classroom. But here I am the manager. How residents behave is my concern, and I assure you that I know everything that happens around here. Nothing escapes my notice and I can tell you that Melanie Lawson is no danger to Mrs Brighouse or anyone else.'

She tapped a pen on the desk. 'You're in Sunnyvale now. You have no responsibilities here, so you can sit back and relax and be confident that I'm doing my job.'

I was being put in my place. A few minutes later I was ushered out her door.

I remembered what Wanda said about Melanie coming from one of the best families in Melbourne. Perhaps Deidre was protecting Melanie, I thought as I returned to my room. Did that mean that she could get away with harassing people, knowing that her misdemeanours would be covered up.

I became angrier the more I reflected on the conversation with the manager. She was trying to bully me and I should have made more of an effort to stand up to her. Perhaps I should have recorded an official complaint about Melanie.

The route to my room took me through the Common Room. The television was on as usual and the woman who waved to me during my tour of Sunnyvale was there with a pile of books. She beckoned me. 'We need to talk.'

I was led to two seats at the back of the room. She looked to see if anyone was nearby and then whispered in my ear. 'I have to warn you. You're not safe here.'

'What do you mean?'

'There have been deaths lately, and that's not the end of it.

When I looked puzzled, she repeated herself.

'Deaths.'

'Whose death?'

'Mr Mora was the first. He was perfectly healthy. Then he was taken up to the hospital and a few weeks later he was dead. Just like that.' She snapped her fingers.

'How old was he?'

'Ninety two. But in good condition. He had just proposed to me. We were going to get married.'

'I'm sorry.'

'Then there was Miss Davenport. There was nothing seriously wrong with her either. But she went up to the hospital, and sure enough, she died last week.' She nodded. 'There's a plot, you see.'

'A plot?'

'People want money but their old relatives don't die. Year after year they remain fit and healthy. The younger ones conspire together. They agree to help each other out.'

Patricia Highsmith had written a novel using this idea. 'You think that they murder each other's grandparents?'

She vigorously shook her head. 'Not them. They pay the nurses to do it. There's a whole group of them willing to do anything for money. And it's simple enough to inject someone with a poison.'

This woman's story was morphing into an Agatha Christie plot.

She looked at me closely. 'You don't believe me.'

'I don't believe that there's anything mysterious about old people dying soon after they're admitted to hospital.'

'But there was nothing really wrong with them.' She looked me up and down. 'You look healthy and you aren't all that old. But I'm warning you. You could be their next victim.'

I couldn't help laughing. No one was going to get much benefit out of my death.

She gathered her books and turned her back on me.

CHAPTER 16

Meg

I FOUND GEORGIA AND WANDA'S COFFEE GROUP WAITING FOR ME OUTSIDE my room. 'We thought you might like to come with us,' said Georgia.

The confrontation with Deidre Barr and the death warnings had drained me, but it was important that I accompany them. They could tell me useful things and a strong cup of coffee would perk me up.

'How are you liking your stay at Sunnyvale?' said Heidi, the former lawyer, once the coffees had been served.

'I've just been warned that I'm in danger of being murdered,' I told them about the encounter in the common room.

'Miss Boyd!' said Georgia. 'Poor you. First Melanie and then Sylvia Boyd. You seem to attract the crazy people in this institution.'

'She's completely bonkers,' Wanda added. 'She thinks this place is full of homicidal maniacs.'

'Her story has changed,' said Heidi. 'Last week she was telling us some of the nurses in the hospital wing were part of a secret society of scientific researchers who are experimenting on old people.'

'They're supposed to be testing dangerous drugs on us.' Georgia smiled. 'And the government is involved at the highest level.'

'They're covering up the fatalities. Removing corpses in the dead of night,' continued Heidi.

We laughed. 'She must get the conspiracy plots from the pile of detective books' I said. 'She's clearly an avid reader. But is it true that she was engaged to a man named Mr Mora who recently died?'

Wanda shook her head. 'Poor man. He was grieving for his wife and Miss Boyd tried to comfort him. I think he found her attentions nothing more than a vexation.'

'At least she's harmless and amusing. Not full of grievances like Melanie,' summed up Georgia.

I was on my way back to my room when Catherine of the Coterie accosted me. She invited me to sit with her in an alcove along the corridor. When we were settled she looked around and then leaned closer, almost whispering. We were so close our faces were almost touching.

'You won't remember me, but I was one of your students back in the 70s,' she said. 'I was a mature age student trying to get a degree in history and I went to your philosophy lectures.'

I didn't remember her but that was hardly surprising. The lectures I gave in those days were often to a class of more than a hundred students. Many took a first-year philosophy course because an arts subject was a requirement for a degree in architecture or engineering. Most wanted only enough information to pass the exam. They weren't otherwise interested in what I had to say.

'I just want to say that I'll always remember what you said about friendship.'

My own recollection was vague. I must have looked puzzled.

'You told us that people remain friends not so much because of characteristics they like in the other person but because of the history of their relationship. I've found in my own life that this is true.' She looked down at her hands, pressed together in her lap.

'I think you're a person who can understand the relationship between Vera and me. We've known each other most of our whole lives. We have a lot of shared history. She supported me through the death of my husband and the loss of our child. I was the person she turned to when her husband left her. The divorce was a terrible blow to her self-confidence. Vera used to be lively, fun loving and popular. She's become bitter and needy. I've probably changed in lots of ways too, not all to the good. But what we've managed to hold onto through all those years and all these changes is our friendship.'

We then noticed Vera approaching from the end of the corridor. The way we were leaning towards each other in quiet conversation made us look like conspirators. I tried to overcome that impression by smiling and inviting Vera to sit with us. She declined with a moody shake of her head. 'Sorry. Catherine and I have to prepare for lunch.'

'I was going to ask you to do something,' said Catherine, 'but it will have to wait.'

CHAPTER 17

Meg

LILA HAD ARRANGED TO MEET ME AFTER DINNER AT A PUB NEAR THE Hampstead post office. It was a chilly, blustery evening and I shivered as I waited for the traffic lights. Why couldn't she meet me at Sunnyvale instead of making me walk so far on a cold autumn evening?

We met near the door. She could see that I was disgruntled and led me to seats in a warm nook near a gas fire. "I'll explain why I brought you here, but first, let's have a drink.'

Lila bought two glasses of the house white and told me her news. Dorothy had managed to get a job as a handywoman at Sunnyvale.

'We didn't think it would be possible, but one of the staff had to go home to the UK because of this virus and she was available to fill the gap. She'll be starting tomorrow.'

I was relieved. Dorothy would be there to support me and I was sure she would make a better detective. She had worked in hospitality for years and knew how to blend into the background. I remember her saying, 'so long as I do my job, I could be a robot as far as most people are concerned'. She would get to know the staff and listen to the gossip.

I shared my encounters at Sunnyvale with Lila. She agreed that Melanie was the most likely source of Sara Brighouse's fear.

'Too bad that manager is a pain. It's clear she won't give us any help.

What you need to do is to talk to Sara. Make her comfortable. Gain her confidence.'

I had an idea about how I could do this, but I couldn't help feeling that Lila would have been more effective. She would have backed Melanie into a corner and made her confess to harming Sara. And she would not have been intimidated by Deidre.

'Miss Barr says she knows everything that happens in the place. Do you think there might be surveillance cameras in our rooms?'

Lila shook her head. 'They put cameras in parking lots and near entrances, but not in private rooms.'

I nodded.

'While you're finding a way of talking to Sara, I'll see what I can learn about Melanie's history,' Lila said. 'Does she have a reputation for violent threats? Maybe there is a police record.'

She also agreed that Miss Boyd's warnings about murder at Sunnyvale shouldn't be taken seriously. 'Just the same, if I have time, I'll see if I can find out whether anyone had any suspicions about the deaths of Mr Mora or Miss Davenport. I can check if the wills are being contested.'

She finished her wine. 'Do you want another?'

I shook my head. 'I want to get back to Sunnyvale before the weather gets worse.'

'I have to tell you why I brought you here. It's a difficult subject,' she waved the glass, 'and I need some courage.'

I watched Lila at the bar, no idea about was troubling her.

She returned to her seat and took a large gulp.

'Have you met a man called Melling?'

I remembered the large man with a wasted body and sunken eyes. 'Yes. He's dying of cancer. He's getting palliative care.'

'I need to tell you about Dan's accident.' She sipped more wine, then began. 'He fell off a cliff. His school had a camp near Healesville where the kids were supposed to learn skills like climbing and bushwalking. Dan was on a weekend excursion with the teacher who ran the sports program. His name was Jim Melling. The kids called him Mighty Jim.'

I nodded. That name could once have been appropriate for the broad-shouldered man she saw hunched over in his chair.

'According to Melling's story, Dan went for a walk by himself early in the morning. He was found near the bottom of a cliff unconscious, his head and back severely injured.'

'You say "according to his story". Do you have doubts?'

'The students weren't supposed to be in the bush by themselves. Dan wasn't the sort of kid to disobey rules. Anyway, why would he get up early to walk by himself when the kids were going to go walking in a group later in the day?'

There were lots of answers I could give. Even sensible fifteen-year-olds sometimes become reckless and disobedient.

'The fact is, I didn't trust Melling. At the inquest he couldn't look me in the eye. And all he wanted to do was to make sure no one could put any blame on him. He left the school soon after. I always wondered if there was something going on.'

'What things?'

'Oh, I don't know. Grooming children, giving school athletes drugs they shouldn't have. I've kept track of him – he went on to teach in other schools around the state and then he worked in the Victorian Football League as a coach. Not long after he started, there was a drug scandal that implicated some of the team members. And then he and his wife were able to buy a large house in Hampstead – much grander than I would think a teacher or a minor football coach could afford. His wife is now dead and then I heard he was dying of cancer.'

'You suspect that Jim Melling was responsible in some way for Dan's fall?'

'I have a gut feeling something happened that was never properly explained. There's no evidence that he did anything wrong. That's what the police said when I wanted them to investigate. They thought I was being unreasonable.'

We sat for a while longer without speaking. A group of people were chattering quietly at the table next to ours.

Lila took another deep breath. 'Remember when we were looking at that brochure for Sunnyvale. I thought the name sounded familiar, and yesterday evening it came back to me. That's where Jim Melling is living. I told you I kept track of him and that's the last thing I found out. I suppose it's not surprising he's there. He's clearly got money if he's been living in Hampstead for many years'

The second wine hadn't eased Lila's anxiety. 'I think he's a bad man.

I wouldn't be surprised if he had something to do with the case we are investigating.'

I was dubious. Lila could tell.

'That's why I couldn't meet you at Sunnyvale. I can't take the chance of seeing him. I gave him a lot of trouble. He'll remember who I am and that could screw up our investigation.'

I didn't think that was likely, but I could understand why Lila didn't want to meet him.

CHAPTER 18

Meg

SUNNYVALE OFFERED AN ACTIVITIES PROGRAM FOR RESIDENTS. A LIST HAD appeared on my bedside table. Scheduled for the afternoon was a piano recital in the common room. I arrived early hoping that Sara Brighouse would attend. And there she was, sitting stiff and upright in a middle row of the chairs laid out for the performance. I quickly took a seat beside her.

'How do you do? I'm Meg Thorne. I'm new here.'

She looked at me as if I had shouted something unintelligible from a long distance. I feared that she wasn't going to answer. But finally, in a voice that was weak from lack of use, she answered. 'Pleased to meet you. I'm Sara Brighouse.'

'Have you been here long?'

She continued looking at me but did not answer. Her son had mentioned that she had come from England with her husband.

'I'm originally from the city of Buckingham,' I said.

Sara's face relaxed. It was as though I had uttered a magic formula. She smiled and a light came into her eyes. 'Yes, I know it. There's a grand estate nearby.'

'Stowe House. My friends and I would sometimes walk up the hill to the grounds.'

'I was born in London. In Camden Town. My mother was a nurse, my father worked for the council. But we had relatives near Buckingham and I got to know the area. Did you know the Petersons? Harold Peterson and his wife Emma. They had a dairy farm near the village of Maid Moreton. They were my uncle and aunt.'

The place name was familiar but I hadn't heard of the people.

'During the Blitz, I lived with them on their farm. My mother came to visit me when she could. Uncle Bert and Aunt Emma grew their own food and they had dairy cows. I remember the milk. I had never tasted anything so delicious.' The memory clearly delighted her.

'When I was a child I only ever saw milk in bottles.'

'They weren't all that far from a lake and my uncle often went down to fish. Once I remember he came back with a trout. My aunt cooked it for dinner. It didn't go far among all of us, but we each got a few mouthfuls.'

I nodded, smiled and leaned closer. 'Do you like it here?'

Her face went blank. No answer.

And then she returned to the farm memories. 'My cousin Mary was younger and she used to take me along to collect mushrooms in the woods. She taught me how to recognise the edible ones.'

Residents were filing into the common room and taking their seats. The concert would soon begin.

'Would you like to have tea with me after the concert?'

'Oh, the tea here is frightful.'

'I know, but there's a café around the corner that serves a reasonable cup of tea. Let's go there.'

'I can't go out.' The rigid expression returned.

'Just for a short time. Fresh air and a good cuppaa will be a treat for both of us.'

'Not today.'

'Tomorrow then.'

She nodded, but as if she didn't know what else to do.

Sylvie was standing in front of the room asking for silence. Next to her was a lanky red-haired young man dressed casually in a blue shirt and tight-fitting brown trousers. 'I am pleased to welcome a pianist who has given us pleasure on many occasions. Johnny Pousset.' She pronounced his surname carefully in the French manner.

There was long applause. I looked around the room. The audience was almost all women. And by their enthusiasm I could see he had a following. Was it a good living playing the piano for old people at care homes? Perhaps he had other engagements as well.

Pousset catered for the age range of his audience. He played music from the Beatles early career, a short piece by Tchaikovsky and then a medley of songs popular in the 40s and 50s. We listened silently as if we were in a concert hall.

When I was a child, my parents used to take me to places where people gathered around the piano and sang songs. My mother sometimes played for them. She had a collection of sheet music in the drawer underneath our piano seat: old time favourites, new songs that had become popular on the radio. But this tradition had long ago died out. We had turned into a generation of listeners.

The pleasant but undemanding music was making me lethargic. I was nodding off. Once again, I had had too much to eat. The applause woke me up. The pianist bowed several times and then asked us if we had any requests. A few people in the back called out titles which he played without hesitation from memory. Then Judy came up to the stage with a piece of paper. She gave us a self-conscious smile and scuttled away.

'A favourite.' He began playing *Blueberry Hill*.

I recalled the words. *I found my thrill on Blueberry Hill*. My mother used to play it.

Suddenly I was aware that Sara Brighouse had become rigid, staring straight ahead with a frozen expression I could not read. Then I noticed Jim Melling in the doorway. He turned and left.

I took Sara's hand. She was initially unresponsive. Then she gripped my hand as if it was the only object she could find to cling to. Was it Melling who had caused her reaction? She was facing the stage. How could she have seen him? Perhaps a peripheral glimpse was sufficient. I kicked myself for not being more observant.

'What's wrong?' I asked, but she let go of my hand and left as the pianist made his final bow to the audience. I tried to follow her as she used her cane to navigate the departing audience. My walker kept colliding with feet and I had to keep up a constant stream of apologies. By the time I was at the door Sara was heading down the corridor.

I caught up at her room. 'Can I help?'

She shook her head and shut the door..

I returned to my room, sat on my bed and thought about what had happened. Was it fear that I had seen in her face? Yes, but there was a stronger emotion: sadness, longing. Had the song caused her reaction? I felt she was living in her past life and the song might have revived painful memories. Perhaps her reaction had nothing to do with what was happening to her at Sunnyvale.

I would get nowhere with the investigation until I could talk to her at greater length.

I needed fresh air. I punched the code for the front door and was thankful when it opened soundlessly. I made my way up the drive, through the gates and across the quiet street to the park. I angled my walker over the kerb and propelled it onto a gravel path.

I was concentrating on avoiding hazards and didn'tt notice where I was going until rounding the corner by the pond, I glimpsed Jim Melling entering a grove of trees on the far side. He was walking fast for someone so ill. I followed, using a row of bushes for cover. As I got closer, I could see a man in a hood half concealed by a tree. Melling slowed; it was an arranged meeting. I watched Melling give his companion an envelope and receive a small bundle. It disappeared quickly into a jacket pocket.

They suddenly turned in my direction, attracted by my noisy walker on the gravel. I pretended that I was simply out for a stroll and focused on the ducks. But I was sure that Melling had seen me looking at him.

I turned the walker and moved slowly around the pond. Would he pursue me or threaten me? There was a couple on a seat near the water, paying attention only to themselves. Their presence gave me some comfort that Melling wouldn't attack me.

I was more sanguine by the time I reached the street. Perhaps Melling assumed that I was merely an old lady, too addle-headed to notice much.

Once safely inside Sunnyvale, I began thinking about what I had witnessed. I had seen this sort of thing before, if only in the movies. It was a drug deal. I was sure drugs and money had exchanged hands. Perhaps Melling was stealing them. I had heard of that sort of thing happening. Residents were given medical treatment and there were drugs of all kinds on the premises. Presumably, he would need a member of staff as an accomplice. Could his activities be the reason for Sara's fear? She might have discovered what he was doing and his response was to threaten her. His appearance at the concert was meant to remind her not to talk.

I called Lila as soon as I reached my room.

Lila gave a satisfied grunt. 'I knew it. He's a suspicious character, and drugs…well, I'm not surprised. . His presence at the place where Sara is being persecuted is no coincidence.'

'But he's dying. He's not going to benefit from a life of crime.'

'He needs money. Staying at Sunnyvale must cost a packet. And who knows? He might have other debts or commitments.'

Lila was convinced that Melling was the reason for Sara's fear. But my inclination to be sceptical of obvious explanations led me to develop doubts. Was there really a connection between Sarah's fear and Melling's presence.

'I can't guarantee that Sara saw him standing by the door. She was staring straight ahead.'

'People often sense things that they don't see.'

Did Lila believe that Melling had a malign presence, like a bad smell? My doubts turned to the park exchange.

'I'm having second thoughts about the drug deal. I saw Melling hand over an envelope and receive a packet. Now I'm thinking it was Melling paying for the drugs.'

'So what? The same reasoning applies. Sara found out what Melling was up to and he threatened her.'

'But would he have cared? People think that Sara is rapidly declining into senility. I've seen that she pays little attention to events and doesn't talk about them. She lives in the past. Even if she could understand what she saw, why would he worry about what she says? No one would take her seriously.'

'He might not want to take any chances. Anyway, her problem may not be senility so much as fear. Perhaps Melling is responsible for her mental deterioration.'

It was no good raising more doubts. Lila was certain that Melling was the cause of Sara's fear. I sighed. 'I still think that Melanie is the most likely source of the problem. Have you learned anything more about her?'

'She doesn't have a police record.' I can make some more calls. Lila sounded bored with that idea. 'You said that Melanie was not at the concert.'

'No. Sara's reaction wasn't caused by Mad Melanie and her cane.'

'That leaves Melling.' Lila sounded triumphant.

'Well, I think we should keep an open mind and consider other possibilities.'

'Such as?'

'The song the pianist was playing when Sarah got that strange look. *Blueberry Hill* was popular in the 50s.'

'*I found my thrill on Blueberry Hill*,' Lila sang. 'But what does a song about lovers meeting on a hill have anything to do with anything?'

'The song was requested by someone at the back of the room. I think it's worthwhile finding who requested it.'

'Very well. Ask around then. It probably won't be difficult to find out. I'm going to learn what I can about Melling's activities since he left Dan's school.'

I put my phone away and stepped outside my room. I could hear voices in the common room. The television was on and an unusually large number of people were watching a news program.

'The coronavirus,' explained Georgia. 'It's spreading through Italy and Spain.' Pictures of people on stretchers and in hospital wards filled the screen. Some of them were attached to ventilators to help them to breath.

Worried chatter followed the news. One of the retired public servants boomed authoritatively from the back of the room.

'There's nothing to worry about. We've seen it all before. Remember the SARS epidemic? A few people died; many were tested. They waved a heat detecting device at you when you got off a plane. But then the virus departed and things went on as usual.'

He was correct; that epidemic had never troubled me or my friends.

My former student intercepted me on the way back to my room. 'I was meaning to talk to you but you disappeared right after dinner.'

We paused near an alcove.

'I was thinking that it would be a good thing – a really great addition to our program – if you were willing to give us a talk on philosophy. Most of our activities are pure entertainment but there are quite a few university educated people in this place and we would appreciate something more intellectual.'

I wondered whether this was true – or Catherine was being selfish. 'The activities program has been fixed. I have a printout on my table.'

'We can always squeeze something in. All we have to do is put up notices, or make an announcement. It's not that anyone around here has a busy schedule.'

I nodded. It wouldn't be hard to prepare and it would give me something else to think about.

'You could talk about friendship.'

I considered for a moment. 'No, I'd rather do something else. Taking Responsibility for Your Past will be the topic. You can put up the notices.'

Catherine seemed unsure. 'That could be very confronting. People here have a lot of past to take responsibility for.'

'So much the better. It will stimulate a good discussion.' I had nothing in mind, but it might provoke a reaction from Melling. There was a small hope that I could help clear up the mystery of Dan's accident for Lila.

Maybe a vigorous debate would also clear Sara's mind. I might learn what was haunting her. In any case, I was stuck for ideas on how to progress the investigation and a philosophical confrontation just might help.

CHAPTER 19

Meg

GEORGIA CAUGHT UP WITH ME AFTER BREAKFAST THE NEXT MORNING.

'Do you want to come and choose a picture or two from my collection?'

Her room was near the reception area. Watercolour paintings in various stages of completion were piled near her bedside table. Underneath the bed was another stack mounted on thin wooden boards or stiff cardboard.

'I'm afraid I'm terribly prolific as an artist.'

'Like Picasso.'

'That's the only characteristic we have in common, unfortunately.'

'You don't exploit women or steal ideas from other cultures.'

She looked at me strangely.

Georgia was not a great artist, but her paintings were much better than her modesty led me to expect. I chose a painting of ducks on the pond and another of the old St. Kilda pier, a place where my parents and I walked when we arrived in Melbourne. Her portrayal of nature was reminiscent of works by the Heidelberg School. I didn't say this for fear she would tell me how much worse a painter she was than Arthur Streeton.

As I left her room, I noticed a visitor talking to Sylvie at reception. When he turned towards me I almost dropped the pictures.

Martin Wilde: the charlatan that Lila, Dorothy and I had exposed was at Sunnyvale. He gave me a quizzical look, hesitated and then turned away for the exit. Sylvie released the door for him.

I was aghast. I returned to my room and sat for a time wondering what I should do.

I had hoped never to see Wilde again. He had to pay a lot of money to people who took legal action against him. The Good Life Centre that was the front for his fraud scheme had been closed. We thought Wilde should have been sent to prison, but the police had not been willing to act. Lila believed he had friends in powerful positions.

Now he was free to exploit more vulnerable people. Was that his plan at Sunnyvale?

The first thing I had to do was to warn the staff. I marched up to Sylvie's desk.

'Do you know that man who was just here is Martin Wilde? He exploited elderly people at his centre in the Dandenongs?'

Sylvie did not seem concerned. 'Yes, I heard something about the healing centre he used to run, some misunderstanding.'

'Misunderstanding?'

'He paid the money back, I understand, and Mrs Wakefield vouches for him. He provides psychological counselling for some of our residents. He's done them a lot good. I hope that you won't go around disturbing people with baseless rumours.'

Back in my room, I immediately phoned Lila. She was less perturbed than I by the news about Wilde. 'Mrs Wakefield probably doesn't know the full story. I'll get Mr Knowles – you know that man who complained to us about Wilde – to contact her. I'm sure he'll be willing to put her straight.'

I was frustrated, but I had done what I could. Wilde was a fraudster and he had been the Grey Ghosts' first case.

Lila knew a lawyer who was acting for a man who had been defrauded by Wilde. Mr Knowles claimed he had a recording with damning evidence. Unfortunately, the only copy had been taken from him by a friend of Wilde's. A courier was to deliver the tape to a city hotel where Wilde was delivering a lecture. We knew Wilde would destroy it immediately.

Dorothy's job was to intercept the packet by posing as Wilde's official representative. She had forged a convincing name tag. Lila was in the hotel lobby in a wheelchair; she had to keep anyone, including hotel security, from interfering with the delivery. My mission was to keep Wilde occupied in the lecture room long enough for Dorothy to accept the delivery.

I remember watching Wilde perform. He knew all the tricks, slowing and deepening his voice for the crux of his message, leaning forward to take the audience into his confidence.

'How can you be truly happy? You can read books, you can try to find the answer by yourself, but your old self will always lead you astray. You need to become the self you have it in you to become. But how can you do that when you don't even know how to begin? Aristotle tells us that we need the guidance of others who know the way and have our interests at heart.'

Poor Aristotle. He would be turning in his grave to be quoted by a conman like Wilde.

Wilde finished spruiking his supposed healing centre and dealt with a few questions. He seemed ready to depart the lecture hall when I raised my hand and stood up. I was trembly but determined to have my say.

I gushed on about how much I learned from his talk and his book, *Putting Enlightenment into Practice.* I had, in fact, skimmed through it. I went on at length about how superior to me he was, as far as enlightenment was concerned. Praise always goes down well and is not likely to be interrupted.

'And you're so right,' I had said, 'that it's hard to get advice on living a good and virtuous life from philosophers. Was it Epi-something who thinks that a good life is a life of pleasure. But it wouldn't be a good thing if people went around all the time having sex and eating junk food. Not that I'm a prude,' I added. This caused nervous laughter from the audience. 'Aristotle thought that participating in politics was a good thing to do. But I can't see that, can you? I mean politicians don't seem to be all that virtuous. But, of course, times were different then. There were also people back then called Stoics who say you shouldn't get upset if your children suffer or if people are treated unjustly. Surely that's not right. I got so angry when it turned out that Father Ridsdale abused children and I'm sure I was right to feel that way. I always believed that

77

Christians were right to think you should spend your life doing good to others but now feminists are saying that women are always sacrificing themselves for others and it's not a good thing.'

The delaying had been going well. No one would be mean to a shaky-voiced little old lady who merely wanted a bit of enlightenment.

Wilde finally managed to intervene. 'Thank you madam for your contribution. Yes, you are right the truth is difficult to find.' He turned away to end the lecture but I hadn't received Dorothy's signal of a successful interception.

'Oh, wait,' I said more loudly. 'I want to ask about Aristotle. You know his golden mean? Maybe there is a bit of truth in all of these philosophies and I'm asking if we can use the golden mean to get to the real truth about virtue and the good life?'

The golden mean was the idea that you act rightly by finding a happy medium between being reckless and being cowardly or being stingy and being profligate. Wilde had looked flummoxed – either because my application of it confused him or because he hadn't got beyond chapter one in Aristotle's book on ethics.

'Well of course we should use any source of enlightenment we can find,' he said. 'But it is important to recognise that you can't become enlightened by reading books. It just makes you confused, as you have so well demonstrated.'

Wilde then recognised that he was making fun of an old lady who was only asking his advice. He backtracked to answer my question more graciously.

'What you say makes a lot of sense and I am grateful to you for asking your question. Of course, I don't ignore what philosophers have said. Philosophy and the Bible are incorporated into my project. But I insist that enlightenment requires other practices besides book learning.'

'Oh, like meditation or psychoanalysis.'

'Yes, a deep inquiry into motivations is part of the process of becoming who you really are.'

My desire to say something rational got the better of me. 'But what if there is no one thing that a person really is?'

He gave me a sharp look. 'Thank you, but I'm afraid we have to end this now. He looked at his watch again. It was almost 10.35, but there was still no signal.

I scooted in front of him as he walked down the corridor, apologising profusely for taking so much of his precious time.

'But is there a way I could learn more before attending the course? Have you written other books?'

He sighed. 'There's *The Key to All Philosophies*. You can order it.' 'Please let me write that down.' I fumbled in my bag and finally extracted a pen and a piece of paper. He looked at easing around me until people streaming from another meeting room made that impossible. I began writing slowly and laboriously. '*The Key*. What?'

'*To All Philosophies*,' he almost shouted.

Then my phone vibrated against my chest – Dorothy's signal.

'Oh, I'm so grateful,' But he was already disappearing down the corridor.

By the time I reached the foyer Dorothy was wheeling Lila out the door.

'I practically had to fake a heart attack to distract the security man,' Lila said when I caught up with them.

'We're good now,' said Dorothy. 'First Wilde will hunt through the crowd for the courier. When he can't find him, he will inquire at the reception. The woman won't know anything because the courier never reached her. The security person didn't see anything because of Lila. He should assume that the courier is late and wait for a few minutes. Finally, he'll call the company and they will have to contact the courier who will be busy driving to another job.'

'Then the shit will hit the fan,' I predicted.

'But by that time, we'll be well out of range.' Nevertheless, she was walking faster and I had to trot to keep up.

'I'll go up to the lawyer's office,' said Lila when we reached the building.

'I'll come too,' said Dorothy.

'I need a cup of tea,' They left me in the wheelchair at the nearest café.

Later, we drank to our success. 'Everything went as it was supposed to,' said Dorothy, who had done most of the planning. 'I was a bit worried there wouldn't be enough time to get my hands on the parcel.'

'No problem,' said Lila. 'Meg put them all to sleep with a lecture on ethics.'

'Yes, of course.' Dorothy turned to me. 'It's your superpower.'

I leaned back feeling warm and happy. I was part of a gang

That warm feeling of accomplishment returned as I sat on the bed at Sunnyvale. The Grey Ghosts had thwarted Wilde once and we might have to do it again. First, we should had to find out what was frightening Sara Brighouse. I did not go along with Lila's determination to make Melling the villain. My job as was to get over any remaining apprehensions about being in a nursing home and find a way of progressing our investigation. I had to find a way of communicating with Sara.

CHAPTER 20

Jenny

SHE FINDS IT IMPOSSIBLE TO SLEEP. SHE IS LYING ON HER BED LOOKING INTO mostly darkness. The light near the bathroom door glows feebly, she can just make out the cracks in the wall. Her eyes trace them again and again from where they start near the ceiling to where they circle around a bulge in the plaster. They form a tubular shape, but she doesn't want to think of what it resembles. She knows that it is something bad. She closes her eyes and tries once more to sleep.

'It's cold in London during the winter. We'll find you a warm coat.'

She and her mother are walking arm in arm along the main shopping street in Melbourne. Her mother directs her to the entrance of a department store.

Their way is blocked. A tall stout blond woman appears out of the mist of an autumn morning like an avenging ghost. She's wearing a cloak pinned together with a silver broach.

'Elizabeth!' The voice is guttural, threatening, ready to curse them.

'Good day, Frieda,' her mother says evenly.

'Where is the diamond bracelet you took from my house? I know you have it. You must give it back.'

Her mother rests her hands on her hips. 'I didn't take that ugly bracelet of yours.'

'You do. And if you don't send it back I'll come to get it. I'm warning you.'

"Don't be silly. If you sort through the junk heap in your bedroom, you'll soon find it.'

'You're a liar, as well as a thief and a cheat. You won't get away with it this time.'

The woman balls her fists and looks like she is about to turn violent.

Her mother is unperturbed. 'Frieda, you're being ridiculous. You're causing a scene.'

They see that the security man at the door is staring at them.

Her mother takes Jenny's arm and directs her through the glass doors.

'A terrible woman!' She bends down to whisper. 'What she's really upset about is that Leo gave her up for me. But look at that ugly cow. Who could blame him?' She straightens. 'Let's go up to the café and have a treat. We can look for coats later.' Her mother puts an arm on Jenny's shoulder and directs her towards the lifts. 'We'll get you some dressy shoes too.'

'What's wrong with the new shoes I gave you?'

Jenny is with her Aunt Josephine at a social function in Toorak. But she has worn the wrong shoes.

'Why do you never wear the clothes I buy for you?'

'But I am,' she says, indicating the silk dress that was bought at the exclusive shop in Hampstead where her aunt did all her clothes shopping.

Aunt Josephine looks Jenny up and down and brushes a fleck of dirt from the collar. 'You're my daughter now and I want us to look like we belong together.'

She guides her to a table where little cakes decorated with icing sugar are spread on a platter. 'Have one of these,' her aunt suggests. But Jenny hesitates. She's bound to get crumbs or icing on the dress and her aunt won't be pleased. She sighs. She hopes she will soon be sent back to the school that Uncle Robert found for her.

The Toorak party dissolves before Jenny's eyes and she is back with Rosie in her mother's flat. Rosie is in disgrace. Her mother has ordered her to leave the house.

'How can she do that?' Rosie asks her over and over. 'I haven't done anything wrong. You know that's true.' Rosie embraces her and weeps. 'Will you talk to your mother? She can't throw me out like that. I took good care of you. What harm have I done?'

Jenny has no answer and weeps too.

'I promise I'll talk to her,' she says.

She goes through the house to find her mother. She hears voices coming from the back veranda and makes her way through the kitchen. Her mother and Aunt Josephine are walking in the garden. It's late spring and the jacaranda are in flower. They stroll down the flagstone path and stop by the pond.

'I don't think you realise how much you are hurting your brother.' Her aunt is used to speaking at public functions. Her voice is clear and carries to where Jenny sits on the veranda.

She doesn't hear her mother's response, but she can tell by her body that she doesn't like the way the conversation is going.

'Before you pull down everything he's worked for, you should do some research first,' her aunt continues. 'You should make sure your plans are feasible.' She sounds like she is addressing a child.

Her mother raises her voice. 'I assure you we have considered everything. Anyway, it's none of your business.'

'It is my business. I'm your sister-in-law now.'

'You've got my brother under your thumb. But you can't boss me.' Her mother flicks a branch away from her face.

'Don't act like a child.' Her aunt's superior tone aggravates her mother.

Jenny's body tenses as her mother raises her arms. If her mother strikes out, she is sure that Aunt Josephine will strike her back. She gets to her feet, ready to call out or to intervene.

Her mother's voice is cold and vindictive. 'You married him for his money and now you're angry because he won't have as much as you expected.'

'I don't like using the word, but it's appropriate for you. You're a bitch.'

Jenny doesn't want to hear any more. She runs inside.

I don't want to hear any more.

She wakes, her head still fuzzy. She's in her bed at Sunnyvale and rain is pattering against the window. She shakes her head, trying to clear it. Her eyes droop again.

'Think of something cheerful,' Sara used to say when she had one of her spells.

Sara is waiting below the clock at Flinders Street Station. Jenny sees her standing a little apart from the crowd in front of the steps. How confident she looks. She holds herself straight. She is looking around at the people approaching the station, but she is not anxious. Her blond hair frames a face with high cheekbones and a slightly upturned nose.

Sara sees her, waves and smiles. Jenny wonders again how this handsome, sophisticated lady could have become her friend. 'I feel so narrow and provincial when I compare myself to you,' she once said. Sara just laughed at her.

Sara is wearing a white blouse and a plaid skirt that shows off her slender figure. When she approaches, she smiles and Jenny thinks once again that she has never seen anyone with eyes so deeply blue. The smile makes her eyes shine, as if they have their own source of light.

They head to a laneway off Collins Street and sit at a lacquered table under the chandelier of a tea shop.

'We've found a nice place to live,' Sara says when their tea is served. 'In Hampstead. We hope to buy there eventually, once we find our feet. Dave loves his school and Len likes his new job.' She takes Jenny's hand. 'I'm so glad that we moved to Melbourne. Having a friend like you made all the difference to me.'

They relax into the cosy atmosphere of the tea shop. People pass down the lane, some looking at the cakes in the window. How pleasant to be here with Sara, Jenny thinks.

Sara takes another sip of tea. 'Your aunt is certainly a grand lady. An English duchess would have nothing on her. I keep seeing her picture in the society pages. You said she adopted you. Do you have much contact with her now?'

Jenny shakes her head. 'Very little. She's a society lady, as you said. Always in the limelight. Neil and I prefer a quiet life at home. She invites us to her charity balls. Sometimes we go but mostly we don't. We're invited to a dinner at the Wakefield home about once a year, but it's not an intimate family gathering. She always has some of her charity's sponsors around the table and my uncle invites his business associates. I'm afraid I'm a disappointment to her.'

She doesn't like talking about her aunt, so she changes the subject. 'What should we do today?' She has been showing Sara the sights of Melbourne.

'Let's go to the Royal Melbourne Show. I read about it in the newspaper. It will remind me of my rural roots.'

Jenny agrees without enthusiasm. She doesn't like crowds. But with Sara beside her she knows she will be all right.

CHAPTER 21

Meg

I ENCOUNTERED JUDY IN THE CORRIDOR ON MY WAY TO BREAKFAST THE next morning.

She was in a hurry, but I called her back.

'Yesterday during the piano concert, you took up a written song request. Can you remember who it was from?'

If she thought that this question was strange, she didn't show it. 'Georgia gave it to me.' Then she skipped off down the corridor.

However, when I asked Georgia about it she shook her head. 'Someone passed the paper from the back. Judy was nearby and I asked her to take it to the stage.

I wondered if there was a point in continuing this line of enquiry, but I had aroused Georgia's curiosity. 'Why do you want to know?'

'Oh, I'm just interested. *Blueberry Hill* was one of my mother's favourites.'

Georgia sang the first line as she sat down at our table.

'By the way,' I said, 'I've offered to take Sara Brighouse to the café this morning, so I can't join you.'

'That's very kind of you. I don't think she gets out much these days. But I should warn you: she's lost her ability to hold a conversation. Her friend Jenny was much better. She sometimes forgot things but she could chatter about most subjects. Then she suddenly got worse and had to be taken upstairs. Perhaps it was a stroke. It's too bad for her and for Sara.' She sighed. 'You never know. It doesn't bear thinking about.'

I wasn't sure that my excursion with Sara to the cafe was going to happen. Her answer to my invitation had been inconclusive. I had knocked on her door several times without getting a response. Given her state of mind, she might not even remember our conversation.

Shortly before 10:30 I tried her door again. 'It's me, Meg.'

There was a long period of silence before I heard an apprehensive voice. 'Who?'

The door half opened, Sara peered around it cautiously, staring at me blankly. Then she smiled and her face was transformed. 'The lady from Buckingham.'

'I've come to take you out for a cup of tea.'

It took her some time to process the information. 'Thank you so much, but I can't go out.'

'But we can go out together. It's not far. And we can get a decent cup of tea.'

There was another long pause. She seemed to be struggling with her thoughts. Finally, she answered. 'Yes, you're very kind, I'll go with you. Is it cold out?'

I waited while she made herself ready. Her room was larger and brighter than mine and I understood why Melanie envied it. It didn't have many home comforts; no pictures or knick-knacks. She had two armchairs and a desk was stacked with neat bundles of papers and photographs.

We laboured slowly down the corridor behind our walkers, passing Jim Melling. The sight of him did not bother Sara.

Deidre Barr was at the reception desk. 'Where are you going?' She rose from her seat as if she intended to bar our way.

'Just around the corner to the café,' I answered evenly.

She stood there as if considering whether that should be allowed.

'You'll have to sign out.' She pointed to a book on the desk. Residents were supposed to sign it when they left the building, indicating their departure time, the length of time they expected to be out, and sign it again when they returned. I had ignored this rule on my past excursions. It was like being at boarding school. But after all, I reasoned, it was supposed to be for our safety. I signed for us. Sara stood by with a blank expression on her face. Deidre made sure I had filled it out properly and then returned to her office.

In the café I directed us to a table at the back and we stowed our walkers in the corner. Sara was beginning to enjoy our excursion. 'It's good to get out.' Her face, regaining the animation that had been awakened by the Buckinghamshire memories. Her smile was almost roguish, like a child who had got away with something naughty.

'Black tea, no sugar,' she demanded. When it came she sipped it slowly with a sigh of contentment.

'During the War, I lived with my uncle and aunt on a farm near Buckingham. We drank tea in their dining room with their neighbours. My uncle and I always drank it black. They had a dairy farm and I still remember the taste of warm milk right out of the cow. Did you know them? Their name was Peterson. They had a vegetable garden and my mother would come and sometimes would take carrots and lettuces back with her to London. There were mushrooms in the woods. My cousin taught me how to recognise the edible ones.'

She had forgotten that she told me this before. But then I realised that giving me information was not the point. She was losing herself in happy memories. She shuffled through them as if she were fingering the beads of a rosary.

I interrupted. 'Do you know Melanie Lawson?

She shook her head.

'Has she been bothering you about your room?'

Another shake.

She returned to her childhood. 'My uncle Bert named one his cows after me. They all had names. I asked him why he didn't name a boy calf after my father, but he didn't answer. Now, of course, I know.' She gave me another mischievous grin.

I needed to divert her. This was my best chance to solve the mystery of her Sunnyvale fears. 'Your friend Jenny. Did you meet her while you lived in England?'

The blank face returned. The pause was so long I was worried she wouldn't answer.

'No, I met Jenny when I came to Australia with my husband. That was five years after the War ended. She was younger than me but we became best friends. She grew up in Melbourne, near where we are now, and she introduced me to the city. She had an aunt and uncle in high society, but there was nothing stuck up about her. We used to go to the Botanical Garden and sit on the bench near the pond. Just to be with each other and talk while our husbands were in the city and our children at school.'

'What did you talk about?'

That look I had seen at the concert returned. Had I pushed too far, stirred up uncomfortable thoughts? Finally, the tumult in her mind resolved itself. The answer came in a whispered rush.

'Poor Jenny! I thought I could help her, but I did her harm. She's being punished and it's my fault.' She gave me a long, imploring look. What can I do?'

The café door suddenly crashed open and Simon Long stomped in with a hearty greeting, 'Hi, all.'

He turned to Georgia's group sitting near the window. 'Hello girls. Enjoying your coffee and chat? I hope you aren't gossiping about me.'

Then he spotted us in the back. 'My favourite English ladies having a nice cup of tea. Can I join you?' he sat down before we could reply. Sara had retreated into her shell again.

'We're leaving,' I told him.

'Too bad, but I was planning to get a takeaway coffee, so I'll walk with you.'

He called to the waitress. 'A latte with two sugars to go, sweetie. Sweets from the sweetie,' He laughed. The waitress grimaced.

'I hear that you're giving a lecture on philosophy in a few days. Trying to elevate us, are you?'

'It wouldn't be possible to elevate you. You're too high and mighty already.'

He gave me a hostile look. 'You think you're something, don't you?'

'Perhaps we have that in common.'

His coffee was ready and I paid for our teas as Sara retrieved her walker. Simon walked alongside Sara all the way back to Sunnyvale, leaving me to trail behind. He kept up a constant patter. Sara didn't look at him and said nothing.

I signed the book and followed her down the corridor. I wanted to continue our conversation, to get her back to where we were before Simon's interruption. I was behind when she opened the door. Sara stopped so abruptly that I almost pushed my walker into her.

Her room was a mess. The pictures that were neatly stacked on her desk were scattered, the wardrobes and drawers opened. Sara's sanctuary had been searched. She gasped. I saw her staring at a silk, blue wrap-around scarf draped over an armchair near the bed. It was distinctive – and it wasn't there when I waited for Sara to prepare for our excursion.

'Is that your scarf? She shook her head. 'Is it Jenny's?'

'Go away.' Sara didn't face me. 'Please go. I can't talk to you anymore.'

The intrusion should be reported, but I felt that would upset Sara too much. She might shut me out permanently. I backed towards the doorway. 'I'm next door if you want to talk again. Get Judy to fetch me if I'm not in my room.'

I had been so close – then Simon ruined the moment. Was Jenny's treatment the cause of her anxiety? I had to go upstairs to see Sara's friend. Perhaps Jenny was still capable of communicating. She could hold the clue that would explain Sara's state of mind.

The upper floors were secure, the lift required a pass and the door to stairs was locked. I considered my options and then saw a nurse approach with linen in her arms. She had her identity card ready in one hand to access the lift.

'Could I come up with you?'

'Sorry ma'am. You need permission from reception.'

I pushed the walker towards Sylvie at the desk, grateful there was no sign of Deidre.

'I'd like to see the facilities upstairs. You never know when a person might need them.'

She shrugged. 'Ordinarily I would be happy to show you around. But due to the threat of this Covid virus, the management has decided to limit visits to next of kin. We do the same in the flu season. There are some vulnerable people up there.'

'It's a shame access is limited to families. Sara is missing Jenny terribly. Couldn't friends also be allowed?'

'We do sometimes make an exception for close friends, but Jenny's son told us that Sara wasn't to visit and her aunt agrees.'

'Her aunt?'

'Yes. Mrs Wakefield is Jennifer Mueller's aunt. She's also her mother – she adopted her when Jenny's own mother died.'

That was a surprise. Sunnyvale appeared to be full of people connected to Mrs Wakefield: the former public servants, Hermione, Martin Wilde, Jenny. How many more residents owed allegiance to Josephine Wakefield?

More concerning was the visiting ban on Sara.

'Why does the family want to separate two old friends?'

'I couldn't say. But Colin's her closest relative. That's his right.'

'Sara very unhappy. Would it be possible to speak to her son? How can I contact him?'

'I really don't think I can give you that information. But I am happy to tell him to contact you next time he comes. He's a regular visitor.'

On the way back to my room I found Dorothy on a step ladder working on a curtain rail. I checked there were no residents nearby, but still made the greeting a whisper.

'Glad to see you.' I could only see the bottom half of Dorothy, the rest of her was wrapped in the curtain.

'Be careful.'

I looked again. The corridor was still empty. 'Do you know that Wilde is prowling around this place? Have you seen him?'

'No, but Lila warned me. She thinks we should meet tonight at the Gardener's Arms. We shouldn't be seen together but if you can be at the post office at 5.30 I'll give you a ride.' She came down from the ladder. 'Do you have your phone?

I shook my head. A mobile phone is not critical to my life. It was often left behind.

'Carry it all the time. If you need me, text or ring me. If you can't leave message at least give me your location. It can help. Anyway, you shouldn't leave your phone lying around at this place.'

'I need to contact Jenny Mueller's son.'

'That should be easy enough. Tell Lila.'

'There's another thing. If a resident wants to get something belonging to someone upstairs, how would they do it?'

'I imagine personal items are taken away by relatives when residents go upstairs, and the rest is moved to the basement. Access to the storerooms is supposed to be supervised. But we're short staffed; I've noticed that residents are sometimes given the key and they don't always remember to lock up when they leave.' Dorothy shook her head. 'Security is lax around here.'

I turned and saw Simon loitering at the entrance to the common room. I raised my voice. 'It's nice meeting you, Mrs Arden. Could you please hang a few pictures in my room when you have the time?'

CHAPTER 22

Meg

It was a warm autumn evening and I enjoyed the walk to the post office. Dorothy was on time it didn't take us long to reach the Gardener's Arms where Lila had reserved a table.

Lila looked me up and down as I approached. 'You're putting on some weight. It suits you.'

I smiled and sat, happy to be free of the walker and old lady habits.

'I talked to Mr Knowles about Martin Wilde at Sunnyvale.' Lila said. 'He's written Mrs Wakefield a letter. I expect that will ensure Wilde's denied access in the future.' She turned to Dorothy. 'How's the job?'

'I spent most of the day getting the washing machine to work. Sunnyvale has shoddy equipment for a wealthy establishment. It looks like someone has been trying to save money by not replacing worn out machines. That's a mistake.'

I told them about the conversation with Sara and the annoying interruption by Simon Long. I also described Sara's shock when she saw the blue scarf in her room.

'Someone is trying to scare her.'

Lila returned to her pet hate. 'Jim Melling could have done it. He could have sneaked into the storeroom while you were at the café. It would have been easy to hide Jenny's scarf in his pocket.'

'But Sara wasn't concerned about Melling when we met him on the way to the café.' I also had to admit that she did not seem scared of Melanie.

Lila shrugged. 'Perhaps Melling thought she was not frightened enough – she needed a shakeup.'

'Simon Long disrupted our conversation. Can you find something out about him?'

Lila made a note but she didn't look interested.

'I think we have to consider the possibility that the reason she's scared is all in her head,' I said. 'Maybe the daughter-in-law is right. Her fear is the result of age and dementia.'

I shared an example about senility involving an aunt in a nursing home in England.

'She kept saying nobody believed her. And that the truth was in the painting. My aunt was pointing at a blank wall.'

Lila wasn't impressed. 'Sara saw something real on her armchair – a scarf that probably belongs to Jenny. Someone is trying to scare her. We suspect that Melling is doing something illegal that he doesn't want anyone to know about. Doesn't that give us the best explanation for Sara's behaviour?'

'Her fear seems to centre on a threat to her friend Jenny.' I pointed out. 'She thinks she caused Jenny harm.'

I told them about my thwarted efforts to get upstairs.

'I might be able to help,' said Lila. 'You shouldn't have to wait for Jenny's son to visit. I've been looking into the family. Colin has a prosperous furniture business. He's also a town councillor, a deacon in the Hampstead Anglican Church and a member of the local football team board. He attends a lots of functions. I should be able to find a way to approach him.'

I was dubious. She was wearing a yellow top with the purple polka dotted harem pants and her lipstick as usual was bright red.

'Don't worry.' Lila smirked. 'I can dress for the occasion – any occasion.'

I decided not to argue.

'That reminds me,' she continued. 'I found some Wakefield family scandal.' She paused for dramatic effect. 'Jenny's mother was shot in her Hampstead flat.'

'That's horrible!' I exclaimed.

'She was killed with a revolver. Jenny was there.'

'Poor thing,' I said.' 'How old was she?'

'Thirteen. No one was arrested.' Lila added.

'Why not?'

'The police decided Jenny shot her.'

'My goodness. That is shocking.' I looked at Dorothy who showed little emotion. 'What else do you know, Lila?'

'The newspapers said there had been reports of break-ins, robberies and even a kidnapping around the flats. Elizabeth bought a gun for protection and taught Jenny to use it. Apparently Jenny heard suspicious noises; she grabbed the handgun and rushed into the room. It went off, killing her mother. Detectives concluded it was accidental – they found the weapon was easy to fire.'

'There was no doubt that Jenny fired the gun?'

One of the servants took it from her.'

'Not much doubt then, I guess.'

'Well, that didn't stop the newspapers from speculating. A gun fatality involving the wealthy Wakefield family was fodder for the tabloids. Stories emerged about regular arguments between Elizabeth and her lover, Leo. Neighbours told reporters they heard him threaten to kill her.

'Elizabeth was often heard arguing with her younger brother about money. They had inherited a thriving business, yet Robert questioned his sister's spending habits. That fortune went to Robert and the woman he had recently married, Josephine – currently the empress of Sunnyvale.'

That made my eyebrows arch. Dorothy looked just as intrigued.

'Did the newspapers dare suggest Robert or Josephine might have been involved?'

'Not directly. I read that Robert was in Sydney on business Josephine's servants told everyone the rising society star was at home when the murder happened. The story fizzled. Reporters found a former friend who had accused Elizabeth of theft and a servant with a grudge. It was irrelevant – the police had Jenny with the gun.'

'The poor lass.'

'What happened then?' asked Dorothy.

'Jenny spent several years in a mental hospital. Robert and Josephine adopted her when she was released as they had no children.'

'That was charitable,' said Dorothy.

'Possibly,' Lila nodded. 'It was also a good way to suppress a scandal.'

'We know that Jenny eventually married and had a son. Now she is back in the Josephine's care at the nursing home she established.'

I did some quick calculations. 'The murder took place almost 60 years ago. I doubt if it has anything to do with the case we're investigating.'

Lila shrugged and gathered her things. 'By the way, I found something about Mr Mora and Miss Davenport – the people mentioned by Sunnyvale's mad crime fiction reader. They died soon after being moved to the hospital wing. But no one thought anything was amiss. Both left money to Mrs Wakefield's foundation.'

'Oh. Why wouldn't that be suspicious?'

'They were Hampstead people – Mr Mora was on the Sunnyvale board and both had been long term acquaintances of the Wakefields.'

That made sense, I guess. Residents often leave money to hospitals and institutions that cared for them.

Lila paused with car keys in hand. 'The money was certainly timely for Josephine's new geriatric centre project. She wouldn't have been able to buy the required land without Mr Mora's money.'

She ushered Dorothy and I towards the pub exit. 'My next priority Meg is to get you permission to visit Jenny.'

CHAPTER 23

Jenny

JOSEPHINE IS SHUFFLING THE CARDS FOR ANOTHER GAME. HER MOTHER IS shopping for clothes for the trip to London.

Her aunt gives Jenny an inquisitive look. 'Do your mother and Leo quarrel?'

She can't answer. Her mother won't like it if she tells the truth and she doesn't want to lie.

'Come now. I'm only curious. All couples have their disagreements.'

'Sometimes,' she says. Leo gets angry and they shout at each other. She worries he might hurt her mother. 'Leo thinks she's too friendly with other men.' The admission brings shame.

Her aunt pats her on the shoulder.

'You don't want them to marry, do you? You think Leo would be bad for your mother.'

'Yes,' she admits. 'But don't tell her I said that.'

'That can be our secret.' She hands Jenny her cards. She is smiling.

Later, Jenny hears Uncle Robert return. She is supposed to be reading in her room, but she hears her uncle and aunt talking in the garden. She wanders out to the veranda.

They are on the path that circles the garden beds.

Her aunt is impatient. 'What did the lawyer say?'

'He doesn't think it will do any good to challenge the will.' Uncle

Robert kicks at the sun dial as they pass it. They reach the end of the garden and Jenny can't hear her aunt.

They loop back towards the veranda. 'That's worth trying,' Uncle Robert says. 'But I don't think I can offer a bribe big enough to make him give her up. Leo thinks he's going to get more out of marrying her.'

They turn the corner but her aunt's is clear.

'If you told her you'll take back all the money you gave her from the business over the years she might think again.'

Her uncle does not respond.

'And another thing. The child. Your sister's not a good mother. That's obvious. She leaves her most of the time in the hands of that Rosie, who's not much older than she is. We could make a case for custody. That might stop her in her tracks.'

'I can't do that to my sister.'

'Your sister! You've always been too good to her. But now you must save her from herself. The child says that the man is violent. Can't you persuade her to think again, at least to delay for a few months?'

'I can try,' says Uncle Robert, but he sounds doubtful.

'We can't allow this to happen.'

'Are you taking the child with you?' The questioner is Aunt Josephine. They are sitting around the dining room table in her uncle and aunt's home. The meal is on the table.

'Of course,' says her mother. 'Why wouldn't I? Jennifer is my daughter.'

'But your life will be very unsettled, even if everything goes well.'

Her mother prickles. 'Leo's brother has found us rooms we can settle into as soon as we get to London. When the money finally comes through, we'll be able to purchase the building we want for our business. It needs a bit of fixing but Leo's brother says there is nothing seriously wrong with it.'

'Are you sure?' says her uncle. 'Have you got someone independent to check the property?'

'Leo's brother says it's structurally sound, just cracks in a few walls.' The questions are irritating my mother.

'You need a proper assessment. Repairs could cost millions.'

'Oh, stop it. You're getting on my nerves. You're not going to change my mind. We're off soon as we're married. We expect to get the money that's owed to me, as soon you can arrange it.'

Uncle Robert grumbles, shrugs his shoulders and turns his attention to his dinner. But Aunt Josephine returns to the subject after the first course.

'Think of Jennifer. She's only thirteen and she's a very shy little girl. How is she going to adjust to such a change in her life?'

'She'll be fine. Won't you, Jenny?'

She dutifully nods.

'Of course, she'll have Rosie,' Aunt Josephine continues. 'They're very close. I see them walking hand in hand. Almost like friends.' She clearly doesn't approve.

'We aren't taking her. Jenny will be going to a boarding school. She doesn't need a nursemaid.'

Her mother leans over and takes Jenny's hand. 'Don't worry dear,' she says. You don't need Rosie. You'll find lots of friends at school.'

Jenny is annoyed, but doesn't protest.

'Where is the school?' her uncle asks.

'Somewhere in Sussex. Leo's brother knows about it. It has a good reputation.'

'You're putting an awful lot of confidence in a person you've never met,' Uncle Robert complains.

'You don't like Leo, naturally you don't trust his brother.'

'All right. I was just wondering. Let's drop the topic and enjoy our meal.'

'I wasn't the one who started it.'

For a few minutes the only sound in the room is the clatter of cutlery.

Aunt Josephine breaks the silence. 'How about her father? Does his family have anything to say about his child moving to the other side of the world?'

'Josie,' warns my uncle.

Josephine ignores him. 'Who is he anyway?' A pause, 'Do you even know who he is?'

Her mother screws up the serviette, hurls it on the table and gets to her feet. 'Jenny's father died in the war, if you must know. I've had enough. We're going. Jennifer, get your scarf.'

Jenny follows her out the door.

When they get back to the apartment she remembers her promise to Rosie.

'Why are you throwing Rosie out?'

'Forget Rosie,' her mother is impatient. 'You're going to a new life. You don't need her anymore.'

'She says you're throwing her onto the street. How can she live?'

Her mother forces Jenny to turn her head so that they are facing each other. 'I am not a cruel woman. But she is wicked. What she was doing with you was a crime. She's lucky I'm not turning her over to the police. I told her that she could go to jail. She has no reason to complain. She's out of our lives and good riddance. Let's not talk about her again.' Her mother gives her a little shake as if to close the topic down forever.

A hand on her shoulder.

'You're having a bad dream.'

She opens her eyes; Nurse Nancy is by the bed.

'Your breakfast will be here soon. Do you want a sedative?'

She shakes her head. Nancy opens the blinds. The sky is grey. Her eyelids droop again.

She is walking down the wide boulevard leading to the arts school where Aunt Josephine has sent her for drawing classes. She sees Rosie approaching from the opposite direction. There is no way to avoid her.

Rosie shouts with joy, rushes up and grabs her arm. Jenny shakes her off. Rosie looks so hurt that she invites her into the school café. Rosie is wearing a shabby sweater, too light for this cold autumn day. She shivers in her seat, lights a cigarette and stirs her coffee without looking up.

'Are you working?'

'I have a cleaning job at a nursing home. But it's not enough. Well-paying jobs are scarce.' Then she leans towards Jenny. 'Your aunt once gave me money. Can you ask her again?'

'No.' Jenny shakes her head vigorously. She opens a handbag and takes out her lunch money and puts it on the table.

Rosie looks like she might refuse it, but then she gathers it up.

'Do you hate me?' she asks.

'No.'

'I still love you, and I never did you any harm. Your mother threatened me with the police. How could she be so cruel?'

Jenny says nothing. What Rosie did was wrong. Jenny knows that now. She can't hate Rosie but she doesn't want to see her anymore. She reminds Jenny of things she doesn't want to think about.

Nancy is talking to the male nurse. Harry has come to give her an injection.

All for the best.

CHAPTER 24

Meg

I FOUND A LARGE GROUP OF RESIDENTS WATCHING TELEVISION IN THE common room after breakfast. People returning to Australia from China and Europe had tested positive for the new virus.

'It's going to spread like wildfire,' said Georgia.

Wanda looked worried. 'It's mostly older people who are dying.'

I preferred to get my information from the newspapers in the lounge. It was dark, I didn't notice Miles Reading until he rose from an armchair. My arrival had interrupted his solitude.

'I'm sorry for disturbing you.'

He stopped in front of me, causing conflicting emotions. I was sorry for him and angry. His perpetually glum face, downcast eyes and the oppressiveness of his silently borne sorrow was becoming unbearable.

I wanted to break the silence but conventional platitudes would be wasted. I decided to be practical. 'Are you taking medication?'

He stared a moment longer. 'No. Not anymore.'

'Why not?'

The hesitation was briefer. 'Pain is something I need to feel.'

My anger spiked. Why did he think that self-punishment could do himself any good? 'Did your wife love you?'

He turned away, then stopped. 'Yes.'

'She would hate you doing this to yourself.'

'Mind your own business!'

I saw the anger as he stormed towards the exit.

'Someone has to look out for you because you aren't doing a good job of it yourself.'

If there had been a door he would have slammed it.

I found Rod Knight, the psychologist, in the common room. I sat down beside him.

'Can I ask you something? Is it possible to condition someone to fear objects that aren't in themselves fearful?'

'That's fairly easy to do,' he replied. 'The pioneer behaviourist, John Watson, demonstrated this with an experiment on a young child. He was given a fluffy toy and at the same time someone made a loud scary noise behind him. After a few repetitions, the child showed fear every time he saw the toy, even when the noise wasn't present. The response was generalised: he reacted with fear whenever he encountered anything fluffy.'

'The poor kid.'

'Yes, they wouldn't allow experiments like that today.'

I thanked him and returned to my room to prepare my philosophy talk. Several times I stepped away from the writing to knock on Sara's door. She didn't respond.

Lila phoned with good news.

'You have permission to visit Jenny Mueller! I told you Colin is involved with the Hampstead Anglican Church. So, yesterday, I went to a service.'

I tried to picture Lila in her Sunday best. Did she wear her rainbow caftan or the skirt with purple flowers?

'He's quite a distinguished gentleman; thinning blond hair, almost handsome, although a bit pudgy. I think he was there with his wife.

'I waited for them by the door after the service. The wife was chatting to another person, which gave me an excellent opportunity to collar him. I steered the conversation towards 'my mother' in Sunnyvale.'

'*Your* mother?' I protested. 'She would have to be in her 90s.'

'Don't fuss. We talked about our mothers' state of health. You are feeble but mentally alert.'

'Feeble?'

'Oh hush, Meg. It helped me develop his trust. He soon revealed that he had no say what facility his mother went to when her dementia made it impossible to remain at home. Josephine Wakefield insisted that Jenny move to Sunnyvale.'

'That's interesting.'

'I got the impression that Colin is ambivalent about the aunt who adopted his mother. Anyway, I spun him a line about how you and Sara were missing Jenny.'

'Did he give his approval for a meeting immediately?' I asked.

'No. Her condition has declined in recent weeks and he was worried she wouldn't recognise her friends. Finally, he agreed to let you see Jenny – but not Sara.'

'Why not?'

'Colin says Sara is a bad influence and makes his mother anxious.'

'That's hard to believe. Sara is lovely – when she engages. Which I'm sure she would with her friend.'

'Colin doesn't see it as a healthy friendship. He said his mother had a tragic childhood and that Sara dredges up memories that are best forgotten. Anyway, the good news is that you can see Jenny whenever you like.'

'Your tactic wasn't ethical, but it worked. Well done Lila.'

'I haven't finished,' Lila said. 'I thought it was interesting that Colin didn't care much for Josephine, so I delved into the business affairs of the Wakefields and their relatives.'

'Yes?'

'Colin's furniture manufacturing company is really owned by Hampstead Holdings – the company Josephine inherited from her husband. That's the source of her money for Sunnyvale and other projects.'

'Like the future Wakefield Geriatric Research Centre,' I said. 'They certainly keep it all in the family. I suppose Colin manages the furniture business because he's Jenny's son.'

'Not quite. Colin established the company but ran into difficulties during the 90s. That's when Hampstead Holdings bought it. They stripped its assets and left a shell for Colin to manage. It's business, but you can understand if Colin resents Josephine Wakefield.'

I shifted the conversation to Dan's welfare. Lila was worried his care facility was talking about limiting visits to protect patients from the virus. I commiserated, but I had a dilemma to solve. I could get access to Jenny Mueller, which might help solve the puzzle with Sara – our mission at Sunnyvale. But I also had a commitment to prepare a lecture. Pride wouldn't allow me to cancel, or deliver anything but my best. I decided the visit to Jenny upstairs could wait.

CHAPTER 25

Meg

I WAS PLEASED BY THE ATTENDANCE IN THE COMMON ROOM. CATHERINE WAS up front, of course, along with Vera without her pearls. Georgia, Wanda and their group filled the middle row. Rod Knight sat near the front. Jim Melling looked like a reluctant attendee. Simon sat in my eyeline, perhaps to sneer. Much to my surprise, Miles Reading had found a seat at the back.

I felt guilty for harassing him. Did the rough treatment do him some good? He appeared to be taking an interest in the world around him. I checked all the faces; no sign of Sara, which wasn't surprising. I was grateful the mad cane woman was causing mayhem somewhere else. One of the former public servants sat in the same row as Miles.

I began my talk with an example.

'A young man of 20, let's call him Schmidt, joins the Nazi SS and participates in killing Jews. He escapes to Brazil. He is now 96 years old. He long ago renounced Nazi beliefs. His interests, attitudes and motivations have gone through a complete alteration, and he feels no connection to the person he was in 1943. The views and behaviour of this person are now alien to him. But is he still morally responsible for the crimes he committed back in the days of the Nazis?'

Those who responded to my question all agreed that he was responsible. Julie, a former lawyer, pointed out that a court would find him guilty if there was evidence of his crimes. A judge might give a person a reduced sentence if he demonstrated remorse or because of the infirmities of age. However, for the crimes Schmidt had committed, she doubted that there would be any leniency.

I continued. 'We believe that a person should be held responsible for whatever crimes he commits during his life, whenever they occurred. We also believe that a person is not responsible for the crimes committed by someone else. But people can change in profound ways during the course of their lives. Scientists tell us that the cells in our bodies change every seven years, and we know that people undergo great changes in their physical appearance as they age. People also undergo psychological changes. They no longer believe what they did when they were young or have the same goals. Some people go through profound changes in their attitudes and commitments. The philosophical question is why we should think that they remain the same person as they were when they were young. And if they aren't the same person, then perhaps old Schmidt should not be held responsible for what young Schmidt did.'

My audience shuffled uneasily.

'Well of course he's responsible,' said a voice in the back. You can't get out of it just by getting old.'

'What if he went insane?' someone else said.

'What if he got a brain transplant?' There was a titter from the audience.

'Well,' I said, 'becoming old is sort of like getting a brain transplant, except that the changes happen gradually so we don't think of it in this way. But when we are old our tastes, attitudes, beliefs and goals are different from what they were when we were young, sometimes profoundly so. If we ignore all the changes in between and look only at the early and late stages in our lives, the result could look rather like we had received someone else's body and brain in place of our own. Memory provides continuity. But sometimes even that fails. And if Schmidt has become so different as a person why should it matter what he remembers?'

'There are deep aspects of personality that are not likely to change in the course of a person's lifetime.' Rod Knight was presenting the view of science.

'I'm not doubting that. I am asking whether that matters when we have to decide whether to hold a person responsible?'

'But I am the same person that I was when I was 20. There's no question,' said Catherine.

'Yes, and I believe that I am the same person I was when I was 20. But why do we believe this so strongly when the physical and psychological facts are so much more uncertain?'

Julie was indignant. 'Where would we be if we didn't believe this? Would a superannuation fund be able to withhold some of the money you put into it on the grounds that your old self is not the same as the young person who put some of it in?'

'A good point,' I said. 'And I think you are on the right track. The answer to the question of identity is not answered by an appeal to science. Our continued identity as a person depends on our existence as social beings.'

My audience was puzzled.

'Think of your relationship to your children and great grandchildren. Whatever changes of personality you have gone through during your life, these relationships endure and are often a central part of your life. You might have had some of your friends since your childhood, and all of you have no doubt changed in all sorts of ways, but what is important to your ability to maintain your friendship is a history of being together. If you value this history, how can you believe that you and your friends are not the same people that you were when you first met? Even Schmidt probably has some friends or acquaintances that he has known since he left Germany and perhaps before.'

There were a few nods.

'But there is another consideration. We are moral beings and we want justice to be done. If the world were just, then all bad deeds would be uncovered and appropriately punished, and all good deeds would be rewarded. But the world is often not just. People die before they can be made to account for their sins. People go to their graves unrewarded for the contributions they have made. Those of us who believe in God think that God will somehow make up for failures that result from the limitations of human justice. A belief in God is a sign of a longing for justice that the world cannot deliver.'

A few people in the audience looked uncomfortable, as people tend to do when you mention God.

'Our ideas about individual responsibility reflect the importance of justice. We are taught as children to take responsibility for our deeds. We are supposed to become the kind of people who can take responsibility for what we do. So long as we are – so long as we are alive and in our right minds – we serve the cause of justice by refusing to give up this responsibility or letting others do so.'

The audience, realising I was done speaking, clapped. There were only a few questions. Someone thought that I had concentrated too much on justice. God was merciful. Surely that should be taken into account.

One of Georgia's group wondered why we had to make restitution to Aborigines since we weren't the ones who did the wrongs. I answered that some responsibilities belong to groups rather than to individuals.

Simon Long put up his hand. 'What if a person does something that he doesn't know is wrong. Should he have to take responsibility for it?' He had the air of someone who thought he was being too clever for me.

'If people really have no way of knowing that their actions will cause harm then you're right,' I admitted. It would be wrong to make them responsible. But in many cases ignorance is wilful or inexcusable. Slave owners in the American South couldn't claim they didn't know that slavery was wrong by ignoring all the arguments against slavery. A man can't say that he didn't know that he demeaned a waitress in a café 'by calling her 'sweetie' when he should have known that many women do find being addressed in this way insulting and demeaning. Ethical responsibility requires overcoming ignorance when that's possible.'

Simon shrugged, got up and walked out of the room.

Questions dwindled after his departure and the session ended.

People nodded to me as they walked out. A few told me it was 'stimulating' – a word people reach for when they don't know what to think. Most people find philosophy puzzling. Why should anyone question what no one would ever think of denying? In their view, I had given what they regarded as an unnecessary answer to a pointless question.

Catherine, however, was gushing. 'Really that was so good. We should do more of these talks in the future.'

I was sure that the appetite in Sunnyvale for philosophy had been sated. The public servant gave me a weary look as he departed and Miles did not even glance in my direction.

Georgia invited me for a drink with her group in the lounge. She brought out several bottles of wine.

After a glass and a half, I needed to clear my head. I trundled across the road to the park to walk around the pond.

It was a bleak day and the light was fading. I was concentrating so hard on where to place my walker, that I didn't see a man approaching until he was directly in front of me.

Jim Melling was blocking my path. His face was a grey, his mouth was set in the grimace of someone in serious pain. Instinctively I drew back. No one else was in the park, no way I could escape. I pictured myself floating face down in the duck pond, my walker stuck in the reeds like an abandoned supermarket trolley.

'I'm not going to hurt you. We need to talk,'

He ushered me to a bench overlooking the pond.

I sat; he stood and glared at me.

'What do you want?'

'I'm telling you. I'm bloody sick of this!' His words came in bursts, as if he had to gather up the energy to get them out. .'You're spying on me. You're up to something with that Lila Galli. You're out to get me. That talk of yours. That's what it was for, wasn't it?' It's harassment and I want it to stop.'

He stopped ranting to take a deep painful breath. 'No, I didn't push her son off a cliff. No, I'm not a child molester. I'm not any of the things she calls me. That's the truth and she needs to accept it.

Melling grasped the top of bench to steady himself. My fear had been replaced by the concern that he might collapse. I indicated that he should take a seat beside me. I waited until he was settled and breathing more steadily. 'Why don't you tell me what happened?'

The silence stretched to the point I thought he would never break it. But then he began talking, staring into space as if he were addressing an invisible audience.

'The school had a camp in the Ranges. Not much. A dormitory, kitchen, common room. We took the kids there to teach then bush skills. How to navigate, how to set up camp. That sort of thing. We taught basic climbing. Perfectly safe. Rope attached to a spike hammered into rock. Always someone at the top and someone below keeping them secure.

He took another painful breath. 'The place was run down. The roofs leaked; rats ran around at night. No money was spent on upkeep. I complained. All of us complained. Nothing happened.

'I arrived that spring with 12 boys. Lila's Daniel among them. It was late in the day but I noticed the climbing rope was still hanging from the cliff. Left there all winter, I reckoned.'

'That was bad?'

'Bad? Ropes can't be left like that. And it had been used all the previous year. It was an old rope that had been left in the worst conditions. No way we could use it. I told the kids there wouldn't be any climbing, just bushwalking.'

First thing the next morning I went to take it down. That's when I found Daniel. Must have decided to get up early and use it before it was taken away.'

'He fell?'

'The rope broke when he was belaying down the cliff. He was lying on the boulders at the bottom. Alive. But his back was all wrong. I feel sick when I think about it.'

'You're saying that the accident was Daniel's fault?'

He shook his head. 'A teenage boy? The real blame belonged to the school. That was blindingly obvious. I told the headmaster I would say that to the police.'

'But you didn't.'

'No. The headmaster said he'd tell them about my use of heroin. I'd never get a decent job again.'

'Heroin!' I thought of the exchange in the park and drew away. A drug addict was capable of anything.

'Yes. Heroin.' He was defiant. 'Not hard to explain. Injured my back playing football years ago. Lot of pain. Thought I would be a cripple for the rest of my life. Heroin was a godsend. If you have a reliable dealer, if you're careful, heroin addiction won't stop you from doing your job.'

I wanted to walk away, but I had to hear the rest of his story. 'You said nothing about the rope.'

'Got rid of the rope. Told the police nothing. Kept my job, but I left the school as soon as I could. Went off heroin. Found another way of coping.'

He turned and stared down at me. 'That's it. That's what happened. That's all I have to tell. Do you believe me?'

One thing he said was clearly untrue. 'But you haven't given it up. The heroin, I mean.'

He glared. 'You spied on me. But why should I care. I'm in pain. Heroin is my choice of treatment. Why shouldn't I have it? Tell the police if you want. Tell anyone. What can they do to me? 'I'll soon be dead.' He crossed his arms.

He was making me cross. The only person he seemed capable of caring about was himself. 'I have no intention of going to the police or telling anyone at Sunnyvale. But Lila should be told the truth. She and her son suffered an injustice and you helped to cover it up.

'I'm not going to go anywhere near that woman You tell her. That's enough. She can stop harassing me.

'No, it's not enough. You know that.

He shook his head, about to stand.

'They called you Mighty Jim,' I couldn't resist saying.'

He looked like he wanted to throttle me. But I had started and I wasn't going to back down. 'You've already said it. You're dying. What does it matter if you tell the world what happened? What can anyone do to you? And knowing the truth, having someone willing to testify would mean a lot to Lila and to the future well-being of her son. Don't you want justice for Daniel?'

'Don't lecture me. That talk was more than enough.'

He settled back onto the bench. We sat in silence. A honeyeater warbled its last song of the day.

'Very well,' he finally said. 'I'll talk to her. Are you satisfied?'

I nodded. I wanted to say that none of this was about me.

He stood, nodded to me and trudged towards the park gate. Then I remembered there was something I had to ask him.

'Have you done anything to frighten Sara Brighouse?'

He stopped, looked at me as if I was crazy. 'I don't even know the lady. Why should I do that?'

Then he continued his painful exit.

I phoned Lila and told her what I learned from Melling. 'If he doesn't contact you soon, I'll remind him. But I think he will. He wants to get you off his back'

'Huh!' It was more of a threat than a laugh. 'If he doesn't contact me, you can be sure I'll find him.'

My thoughts turned to Sara. I tapped gently on her door. She didn't respond or turn up for dinner.

Lila arrived at Sunnyvale the following evening in her brother's car. We found a quiet area in the lounge.

'He contacted me,' Lila said. 'We talked.'

'Do you believe him?' I asked.

'I think he was too keen to tell me how little responsibility he had for the accident. But I think he's telling the truth.'

'What will you do?'

'I've made an appointment to talk to our lawyer friend. If the Church can be held responsible for abuse to children that happened many years ago, then I don't see why it can't also be held responsible for what happened to Dan. Melling was reluctant to bring things out in the open, but he finally agreed to make an official statement.'

'You'd better get it recorded soon.'

'Yes. I hope his testimony results in a trust fund for Daniel.' She held my hands. 'Thank you. I don't think this would have happened if you hadn't given him a push.' She sighed. 'I also have to accept that Melling probably has nothing to do with the case we're investigating.'

'How about Simon Long? Did you find anything about him?'

'No,' she admitted. 'It's a common name, but nothing that fits his age or description. It's weird that every search drew a blank. I'm beginning to think that this Simon Long doesn't exist.'

'Do you think he's here under a false name? He's exceptionally spry for someone supposedly suffering from a muscle wasting disease.'

'Maybe. There could be more than one secret agent in this place. Keep an eye on him. You might find something that will help my online searches.' She shouldered her bag. 'Good luck with Jennifer.'

CHAPTER 26

Jenny

IT IS STILL DARK WHEN SHE WAKES, THE BULGE ON THE WALL BARELY VISIBLE.

She doesn't want to think about what it looks like. Her eyes close again and find Sara.

They are standing near the entrance to the show grounds and people are milling around.

'Do you want to see something typically Australian?' Sara draws her to the wood chopping contest.

A muscular man is attacking a log with an axe. He swings it hard and fast, each whack makes a cracking noise. The cut expands and deepens.

Jenny thinks she can see blood in the gap and she feels ill. She can't watch the axe rise and fall, yet turning her back doesn't block the noise.

She pushes her way out of the crowd. There is a bench a short distance away and she sits with her head in her hands. People pass around her; some stare, curious.

She breathes deeply as Sara told her to do and looks up. Her friend is stepping quickly through the crowd.

'Are you all right?'

'I felt a little queasy. I'm fine now.'

'There's a place to eat nearby where we can sit. Do you feel up to it?'

They walk hand and hand to the building where a group of women from the country are serving food.

'How would you like a vanilla slice?' says Sara.

'How would you like a nice egg on toast?'

Nancy puts the plate down on the table and opens the blinds. 'Blue sky today. It's warm for March.'

CHAPTER 27

Meg

THE NEXT DAY I WENT TO RECEPTION AND TOLD SYLVIE THAT I HAD permission to visit Jenny Mueller. She checked her book and then gave me a quizzical look.

'It says that Mr Mueller, the son of Mrs Jennifer Mueller, has given Mrs Thorne, the mother of Lila Galli, permission to visit her. According to our records you don't have children.'

I shrugged. 'Someone obviously made a mistake, but it's clear I have permission.'

She continued to look at me dubiously. 'Because of Covid-19, we don't encourage visitors in our upstairs facilities. Many of the people there are frail. You can go, but we need to be sure that you take precautions. Nurse Yo will instruct you.' She pressed a buzzer.

Nancy Yo took my temperature, watched me while I fitted a mask on my face and squeezed my hands into plastic gloves. The mask was too large and cut off the bottom part of my vision.

She accompanied me to the lift. 'You must distance yourself by a metre and a half from the patients and staff at all times.'

We entered a large ward separated into cubicles. Each was inhabited, the patients lying prone or propped up in their beds. There were individual televisions, but few were watching or listening. Aside from a row of easy chairs in the corner, the space was entirely functional – no pictures of landscapes or sunny alcoves to enjoy.

A wild-haired woman in a blue nightdress leaning heavily on her walker shuffled towards me.

'Are you the lady from the council?' she asked me imperiously. 'You're supposed to fix my...' She stopped, unable to remember. 'There's something, I know. You need to fix it.' Her agitation made her shake.

Another nurse appeared. 'Mrs Bell, please go back to your room. I'll give you a nice cup of tea?'

The woman hesitated. She didn't want to waste an opportunity with the council lady. – me. 'You should have done it long ago.' The nurse gently coaxed her away.

A scream echoed through the room. It sounded like an animal caged in a zoo.

A man in a nearby bed cried out for a nurse. 'Help me, please. I'm all wet.'

It occurred to me that Catholics were wrong about purgatory. It was not something you went through after death. It was what you had to endure before death, after losing your ability to function. The blessed were those who died before this happened to them. I thought again of my mother in her final months: frightened, confused, beyond comfort. What had anyone done to deserve this?

Nancy Yo guided me beyond the ward to a hallway lined with doors on both sides. She opened the nearest one. 'Here's Mrs Mueller. Remember, keep your distance, and don't stay long.' Then she rushed off to attend to other patients.

Jenny looked almost youthful. Her red hair still had most of its colour. Her face was haggard but not deeply lined. She opened her eyes when I sat on the chair.

'Hello. I'm Sara's friend. She can't visit, so she sent me. She wants to know how you are.'

Jenny's mouth moved but no words emerged. I ignored the new contact rules and reached out to touch her fingers with a gloved hand. The need for human contact was instinctive. She grasped my hand, pulling me closer.

'Sara!' she said. She thought I was her friend, an understandable mistake with her confusion and the mask covering most of my face.

We silently held hands. I didn't know what to say.

At last, she smiled. Her face looked younger.

'I knew you would come. Do you remember what I told you?'

'Remember what?'

Jenny shook her head in frustration. 'You must remember.' She struggled to raise herself, flopped back. 'It's so difficult. I can't think. But I did what you asked and I gave it to you. It's all there. Do you remember? I told you.'

She drew her face close to mine. 'The important thing…' She went rigid. 'They're coming.' Her hand slipped from mine. Her final words were whispered. 'The drawer was empty.'

I sensed a presence behind me. Standing there was Josephine Wakefield swathed in a purple shawl, her hair piled into a bun. She held a cane, but appeared unbowed by her age. Jenny turned away.

'Good morning, Mrs Thorne.'

I tried to return the icy greeting, but was cut off.

'I see that you have been kind enough to call on Jenny. I don't really understand why you have taken the trouble. But as you can see, she is not able to continue her conversation with you.'

I wasn't sure if her formality was put on to mock me, or part of her regal personality. Jenny's eyes were clamped shut.

'I'm afraid Jenny has always been a very troubled person. When she began to fail, I naturally thought that Sunnyvale would be a good home for her. But I fear this has not proved to be true. Unfortunately, she has been encouraged to indulge in delusions that are quick to find a place in an unstable mind. The result is what you see.' She gestured at Jenny who was rigid.

The matriarch's manner made it clear that she didn't expect me to talk. I wouldn't be cowered. 'She has a friend who is concerned about her wellbeing.'

'We don't encourage visitors up here.'

Josephine pursed her lips, tapped the floor with her cane and moved closer. 'There's another matter I need to raise with you, Mrs Thorne. I understand you have been questioning the suitability of Mr Wilde's visits. Martin Wilde is a long term acquaintance of mine and has helped me in some of my charity work. I have complete trust in his ability and probity. I strongly advise you and your friends against pursuing your vendetta against him. If you expect to remain at Sunnyvale, you must respect my judgment about who is a proper person to care for our residents.'

I wanted to argue, but realised it would be pointless. If a lawyer couldn't persuade her, she was unlikely to listen to me.

She turned away. 'Good day, Mrs Thorne. Harry will escort you out.'

A tall, short-haired, heavily built man in a white cape stepped towards me. Harry the henchman. His expression was neutral, although I had no doubts he would carry me out if necessary.

I felt Josephine's eyes on me as I returned through the ward. Harry directed me into the lift, punched in the code and pushed the button. When its door opened to release me in the world below, I felt relief and exhaustion as if I had emerged from Dante's inferno.

CHAPTER 28

Meg

THE CONFRONTATION UPSTAIRS WAS DRAINING, THAT WAS ENOUGH TENSION for the morning. Then I saw Martin Wilde. He was approaching from the common room. Hermione was holding his arm and smiling at him adoringly.

'I'm so glad you are here,' I heard her say. Wilde gave me another puzzled look. I'm sure he was trying to guess where he had seen me before.

I was instantly worried about Hermione; the woman Georgia called the angel of Sunnyvale. Was Wilde trying to extract money from her? I didn't know how it was possible, but I was sure he was up to no good. What could I do to stop him?

I had to talk to Deidre Barr. She was directly responsible for the welfare of all residents. Josephine Wakefield trusted Wilde because they were both part of the Melbourne establishment. Deidre, I thought, would have to be more objective.

I paced my room, gathering the courage to act. Deidre frightened me. She was cold, dismissive and, I sensed, vindictive. I didn't want her to think I was an enemy, detdrmined to make trouble at her establishment. That would be bad for our investigation – and for me. I wanted to avoid her, but I had a moral duty. I couldn't leave Wilde free to exploit vulnerable people.

I braced myself and trundled to reception. 'I would like to see Deidre,' I told Sylvie. Part of me hoped that she wouldn't be available. Deidre emerged from her office, scowled and directed me inside.

I told her almost everything I knew about the conman, only leaving out the Grey Ghosts' role in exposing him. I explained that a relative had been exploited by Wilde and had joined the class action.

She listened without expression. When I finished, she picked up a file from the desk and paged through it.

'I see you have shared these allegations with several people at Sunnyvale: Sylvie, Mrs Wakefield, probably others I haven't heard from yet.' She dropped the folder. 'Now to me.' Paranoia is a common symptom of the onset of Alzheimer's.'

'Paranoia is the belief that people are out to get you,' I replied. 'I am concerned about the wellbeing of other residents.'

She shrugged. The distinction did not make a difference to her. She had classified me as delusional.

The corners of her mouth attempted a smile. 'Relax, Mrs Thorne. I have the best interests of Sunnyvale at heart. I see everything that happens around here, and if someone does something suspicious I will know it. I've told you this before and now it seems I have to tell you again. I'm in charge here, so please leave me to do my job as I see fit.' She gave me a hard look and then turned her attention to a stack of papers in a tray on her desk. As I stood up I saw they had a dove logo at the top.

She saw me hesitate and waved me away. 'Have a nice day Mrs Thorne. And don't forget, I have my eyes on everyone and everything in this place.'

Her statement was more ominous than reassuring. I calmed myself with a cup of tea in my room.

By late afternoon most of the residents and staff were watching the news in the common room. There was no sign of Josephine Wakefield or Simon Long. Judy dashed in and out between the jobs.

The mood was sombre. People were dying in Italy, Spain and the UK. Australia had closed its borders to visitors but it couldn't halt the spread of coronavirus. It sneaked in with Australians returning from overseas. The World Health Organisation had declared it a pandemic.

'At least it's not so bad here,' said Wanda.

One of the public servants shook his head. 'There's going to be a lot more deaths. That's inevitable. Once a pandemic takes hold, there's no stopping it.'

'Are we in danger?'

'Of course. Look at all the people in nursing homes who have died in Italy, Spain and New York.'

'They say that some of the dead are just left in their beds because no one has time to remove them.'

'There's not enough ventilators to go around in hospitals, some people simply have to be left to die.'

'If you're over 70 it's bound to be you.'

'I suppose that's fair. Young people have their whole life in front of them.'

'They're also the productive ones,' said the public servant. 'The old are just a drain on economic resources.'

'Well, I don't like being regarded as just a drain on economic resources,' said Wanda. 'I'm a person. I have a right to life.'

'But if push comes to shove...'

Wanda looked at me as if expecting a philosopher would have something to say, but I had other matters to think about. In a classroom I sometimes asked students whether it makes sense to claim that every individual has an equal worth when it is obvious that some people have superior talents and contribute much more to the common good. But in an emergency it is obvious that this issue is more than merely academic, and I was thrown back into my reflections on old age and the inevitable decline that goes with it. I needed the tranquillity of the park to reflect on my recent experiences.

As I passed reception I noticed there was someone in the office. Not Sylvie, who was serving tea in the common room, or Deidre, who was keeping an eye on residents and the television. I moved to other side of the desk to get a better view; it was Simon, half hidden by the door frame. He was using a small camera to take pictures of something on Deidre's desk. He must have sensed my presence because he looked up. I turned away, pretending to be an old person intent on the difficult business of punching in a code and navigating her walker through the doorway.

At the duck pond, I thought first about my encounter with Deidre.

What else could I do to stop Martin Wilde? Should I try talking to the retired public servants? Should I write a letter to someone on the Royal Commission of Enquiry into Aged Care? I eventually decided to phone Lila and discuss the matter with her. Maybe she could get the lawyer who hired us to send another warning. Mr Knowles might have better contacts.

I turned my thoughts back to the main mission. What was the source of Sara Brighouse's anxiety? Jenny hadn't been able to tell me much. She was clearly heavily drugged and only her belief that I was Sara roused her enough to say a few words. She might have said more if Josephine Wakefield hadn't interrupted.

At least I now knew that Jenny had told Sara something important. Sara might remember – if I could get her to talk again. I had to get past the fear that was keeping her silent and confined to her room.

I wondered if Martin Wilde might be involved. Was he connected with Sara and Jenny? Josephine said Jenny had a troubled mind. Did she receive counselling from him? That wasn't improbable given the Wakefield and Wilde social connections. If so, Wilde would know about Jenny's relationship to Sara. Perhaps he was responsible for making Sara afraid. But why would he do it? What could he gain?

Then there was Simon Long to consider. Taking pictures in the manager's office wasn't his only suspicious activity. Lila's failure to find information about Simon might mean that he was there under an assumed name for a clandestine purpose. He had interrupted Sara and me just when she was about to tell me something important. He could have been responsible for Sara's fear at the concert and he had the opportunity to plant Jenny's scarf in the room.

Somehow all these facts must fit together, but I couldn't think how. Perhaps he was stealing from Sunnyvale. Did Jenny see him? Had she told her friend, but then suffered a mental breakdown and Simon was scaring Sara to prevent her from telling anyone?

I returned again and again to the same questions; it was clear I couldn't answer them.

CHAPTER 29

Meg

'Guess what?' said Georgia when I took my place beside her. I was late because I had to search for a scarf. 'Vera's pearl necklace has gone missing. She couldn't find it after watching the television news.'

'She probably forgot where she put it.' I thought of my own problem finding the scarf.

'She was certain she left it on top of her dresser. She's positive someone has stolen it.'

The missing necklace had replaced the virus as the main topic of conversation. Only Miles, glum as usual, had nothing to say. He usually kept his head down while eating his meals. Lately I had noticed him staring at me in the common room and when we passed in the corridors. I found it unnerving, but at least he didn't seem angry.

Deidre intercepted me on my way back to my room after dinner.

Sylvie was a few paces behind. 'I'm afraid I must tell you that Vera thinks you took her necklace.'

'Why would she think that?'

Deidre took over. 'She says she left it on her dresser after lunch. Everyone was watching television, but you left early. I can confirm that you exited the building at 4.30. When she went to dress for dinner, the necklace was gone.'

Sylvie was embarrassed. 'We just need to look in your room. It's only a formality. It quite often happens around here that things are misplaced.'

'I was in the park,' I protested. I tried to think. Were there other people near the pond? Any witnesses I might be able to call on? I had a bad feeling: Deidre and Sylvie were going to find Vera's necklace in my room.

I was terrified the police would be called. Or would they throw me out. A picture of my expulsion from Sunnyvale flashed through my mind, Deidre standing guard before the entrance like the angel with a sword before Eden. But what could I do?

I remembered the mobile phone in my pocket. I was following Dorothy's instruction to always carry it.

I took a breath and managed to smile at Sylvie. 'Certainly, you can look in my room. I didn't take the necklace but I understand your position. But could you just wait a second. My friend Lila sent me a message during dinner. It's rather urgent. Would you mind if I take the time to text her back? It won't take long.'

Sylvie nodded and I took out my phone. I was nervous and had a hard time finding Dorothy's number. I could almost feel waves of impatience and suspicion radiating off Deidre. I tried to calm myself by breathing slowly. The number came up. I typed.

room search

I then pressed Send. Relief was quickly replaced by a feeling of futility. Could Dorothy do anything?

I leaned heavily on my walker and limped behind it, pretending that my slow gait was the result of disability.

Miles passed us, bemused by the official procession.

Deidre went clicked the light switch. The room remained dark. Dorothy appeared with a ladder under one arm and a box of tools.

'There's a problem with the electricity in this corridor. I think I've located it. It's in here.' She pointed at my room.

'You can't go in there. We're supposed to be conducting a search.' Deidre stood with hands on hips.

Dorothy propped the ladder by the door and put down the tools. 'You can't search without any light.'

Nearby residents began poking their heads out of their doors to complain about the outage. Sylvie went to talk to them. While Dorothy and Deidre argued, I slipped into my room.

I had shut the curtains before going to dinner. Dorothy was buying me time with a detailed explanation about voltage and short circuits. The necklace would be somewhere obvious. I went to the bedside table – they were draped over a book.

The conversation was coming to a climax and Dorothy was slowly manoeuvring the ladder into the room. Where could I put them? My only pocket held the mobile phone. Anyway, Deidre would probably insist on searching me. There was only one thing to do. I used the scarf to pick up the pearls and moved to the window. Dorothy was setting up the ladder, Deidre was in the doorway. I swung open the curtains as if to provide more light.

'Could you hold these tools a moment?'

Deirdre grunted.

I always keep the lower window open a fraction for fresh air. I eased the pearls through the opening. They fell into the garden.

'There that should do it,' Dorothy said. 'Can you pass me the bulb?'

Another grunt from Deidre.

There was a bush below my window which should hide the pearls until I could find a way to secretly return them to Vera. A movement near the birdbath caught my eye, but I couldn't be sure if it was a resident or animal. I breathed deeply and turned around.

'That's fixed. I'll turn on the switch for this corridor and you'll have some light.' Dorothy folded the ladder and marched out.

Deidre was indignant. 'Bold as brass that woman. Treated me like her servant. We should get rid of her.'

'But she was the only one person who could fix our old washing machine.'

The light came on. The search began. As they went through my drawers I couldn't help thinking about the mess I had left after looking for my scarf. My mother told me that I should always wear clean knickers in case I was hit by a bus and had to be taken to hospital. Perhaps she should also have told me to keep my drawers tidy in case the police or other officials wanted to frame me as a thief.

After going through the drawers, they looked in the suitcase in the wardrobe and then came around to my side of the room. Deidre pulled open the table drawer, rummaged through it and then bent down to look under the bed. She came up red faced. She moved a hand around the side of the mattress, looked under the pillows and felt around the side of the easy chair. Her frustration was obvious.

'Do you want to search me as well?' I was standing with my arms folded in the middle of the room.

Sylvie was now deeply embarrassed. 'No of course not. We're terribly sorry to trouble you like this.' Deidre didn't look a bit sorry. She glared at me suspiciously and this time she had cause.

I flung myself onto the bed when they left. After a moment I roused myself and texted Dorothy.

Saved. In the garden.

CHAPTER 30

Jenny

IT IS DARK AND JENNY CAN'T BREATHE, AS IF SHE'S IN DEEP PIT AND CAN'T see the sky. Cold walls push against her. She would scream if she could catch her breath. There's a dim light and she sees the legs of a huge spider spread out against the wall. In the middle lurks its bulbous body. She tries again to scream but all that comes out is a pathetic croak.

'Jenny,' a voice says. 'Jenny, what's wrong? I'm right here right beside you. Give me your hand. I'll hold you. Put your head down and breathe deeply.'

She knows it's Sara, calming and reassuring.

They are sitting on the bench in the Botanical Gardens. A lawn spreads in front of them, Jenny feels like she has been running, Sara has an arm around her shoulder. A mother and child wander past and give them a curious glance.

Jenny opens her handbag, takes out tissues and wipes her mouth.

'I'm fine now. I'm sorry.'

'Don't apologise. You don't have to say anything. Let's sit here and enjoy the view.'

They are on a hill, in the distance she can see the city skyline. She is safe with Sara beside her.

'I'm doing what you suggested: writing what happened.'

"Do you think it helps?'

'Yes. I'll show you when I've finished.'

Sara squeezes her hand. 'Whenever you are ready.'

Jenny wakes, she's in bed. Her heart is beating rapidly but she feels calmer. The walls have receded and she can breathe.

I am Jenny Mueller. Sara Brighouse is my friend. She promised to come if I needed help and yesterday she did.

The joy of seeing Sara at her bedside fades – her aunt chased Sara away.

Jenny manoeuvres the pillow under a shoulder so that she can reach the bedside table. She fumbles in drawer until she finds a photo, the last one taken of Sara. She's standing under a fig tree in the garden, a straw hat in hand. It's hard to see Sara's face in the shadows. Jenny presses the photo against her chest and lies back to wait for morning.

A woman is at the window. Not Nancy. The blinds open. Jenny can see that she is wearing a blue blouse and woollen skirt, her brown hair is cut so short that the nape of her neck is visible.

'Good morning, Mrs Mueller.' A breakfast tray is set on the table.

Jenny recognises her. She sometimes comes in with Harry, the nurse who gives her the injections. One time she was with her aunt. Another time she was talking to Colin. She is a frightening figure. Jenny doesn't like her.

'How are you feeling?' A smile appears briefly as she straightens the pillow, then her face sours.

'Mrs Wakefield tells me you had another visitor yesterday. Do you know who she was?'

Jenny remembers that she is holding the picture of Sara underneath the bed covers.

'Do you know why she visited? What did she have to say for herself?' The woman glares.

Jenny is frightened by her intensity.

'She held my hand.'

The woman is peeved. 'A breach of the rules. She should have known better.'

'Where is Nancy?' Jenny asks.

The woman doesn't answer. She stands by the bed, hands on hips, as if dealing with a naughty child.

'We are threatened by a deadly disease and have to follow strict rules to avoid the spread of infection. No touching. No hand holding. If those rules are broken, you and other people could die. Do you understand?'

'I'm afraid from now on we are limiting visits to close relatives. Your son and Mrs Wakefield can visit you. They know the rules. But no one else. Do you understand? This is for your own good.'

There's no reply from Jenny. 'Good day, Mrs Mueller. Nancy will come to pick up your tray.'

The unwelcome visitor is gone and Jenny feels under the covers for the picture. The light is better and she can see Sara's face. She is standing tall and straight as always. Her long grey hair frames her face. That confuses Jenny.

She tries to remember the woman who held her hand. A mask covered most of her face, but her white hair was short and wavy. Her eyes were light blue, almost grey, not deep blue like Sara's. The woman hadn't been much taller than the top rail of the bed.

She stares at the picture again but she can't turn Sara's image into the person she saw near her bed. So not Sara. Someone else. Sara isn't allowed to come any more, but she sent someone else to see her.

Jenny's spirits lift. Sara has not forgotten. She sent a messenger. And the woman was brave and kind. She held her hand and stood up to her aunt.

CHAPTER 31

Meg

I DIDN'T GO TO BREAKFAST THE NEXT MORNING. I COULDN'T FACE VERA OR any questions about the room search. I was innocent. There was nothing I needed to answer for. But I suspected that not everyone believed this was true. If I followed the example of the Stoic philosophers, then I should be indifferent to others' opinions of me. But I felt vulnerable after an almost sleepless night. I needed time to regain my equilibrium. I made a cup of tea and sat down with my book.

Mid-morning there was a knock on the door. Judy appeared, glanced at me nervously, handed over a bouquet of flowers and rushed away before I could thank her. I was left holding a bundle of purple hyacinths. I looked at the card attached: 'So sorry, please forgive me, Vera.' I looked in my cupboard and found a suitable vase. As I was arranging the flowers, I heard a tentative knock.

Vera, unable to look me in the eye, stood on the threshold. She stepped back as if she were preparing to leave at the first sign of displeasure. I could see that she was doing something extremely difficult. She was humbling herself before me.

I invited her in and sat her down in the chair by the window. 'I suppose you've heard that my necklace was found by the cleaners this morning in the dining room,' Vera said. 'On my chair. It had slipped behind the pillow I use to support my back. The clasp was damaged so I suppose it fell off when I turned my head and I didn't notice.'

'I'm glad you found it. And thank you for the flowers.'

'The strange thing is that I thought I took it to my room after lunch and left it there. But I'm so anxious. All the news about that virus – I can't get it out of my mind. I'm sure it will come here next and we'll be the ones wheeled out in coffins. My mind keeps going off in all directions, and I can't remember the simplest things. I must be confused about what I did with the necklace, mixing it up with what I did yesterday or even the day before.' She paused. 'Do you think I might be getting Alzheimer's?'

I felt sorry for her. It originally occurred to me during my restless night that she might have put the necklace in my room. But her manner was so apologetic, and her effort to understand the mistake she believed she had made was so genuine, that I had no choice but to accept.

But I wasn't going to let her off too easily. 'Why did you think I had taken it?'

'You left the common room when we were watching television and almost everyone else was there. Then Judy told me she saw you in the corridor near my room.' She hesitated. But the resolve that brought her to my doorway finally had its way. She met my eyes for the first time.

'I wanted to believe that you took my necklace. I wanted you to leave. Cathy is such a clever person and she is better than me at practically everything. I was always the popular one at school. The boys found me attractive. But well, look at me now – discarded, old and ugly. Cathy is the only real friend I've got. And it was obvious as soon as you arrived that she was attracted to you. She admires you. She can talk to you about things I can't understand. You are more like her in every way. So why shouldn't she come to like you better?'

I threw up a hand in protest.

'I know this sounds like I'm just trying to excuse myself. But I was frightened of you. I wanted you to go away, and I imagined that you felt the same about me. I was ready to believe that you had stolen my necklace just to hurt me.'

I reached out, taking her hand. 'Catherine is devoted to you. Don't you see that? If you think that she would abandon you, then you really must be going senile.'

We laughed. The mood lightened, and I told her what Catherine and I believed about friendship. I had not offered her a cup of tea but now I thought we both needed one.

We silently watched a flock of sparrows at the birdbath in the courtyard, flitting from one surface to another in search of food. The sky was azure blue and cloudless.

Vera put down her cup. 'I hate to admit it but I'm really scared about this coronavirus. You see on television coffins lined up near hospitals in Italy and Spain and even New York. Everyone knows it kills old people and here we are, sitting ducks. If it gets into this place a lot of us will die. Cathy says it's ridiculous to worry. She's so fearless. But I can't help thinking about it and I have nightmares about being on one of those machines.'

'Most people recover. Even the old.'

'But I can't help thinking that I wouldn't be one of those. I'm overweight and diabetic.' She looked at me earnestly. 'You're fearless like Cathy. And you're a philosopher. Tell me how you do it. How can a person overcome fear?'

I told her that I was no better at it than anyone else, but ancient philosophers liked the Stoics had good advice I always tried to follow.

'Marcus Aurelius says that we should live in the present – because that's what we actually have. We shouldn't pine about a future we may not have. He thought that people who worry about what the future holds are forgetting how to live right here and now.'

Vera brightened. 'Yes,' she said. 'I should always look on the bright side and after all a person can't give up hope. If we get through this, I want to get out of here, travel, do interesting things and maybe I can even find romance.' She hugged herself.

When people find that I am a philosopher, they sometimes ask me about the meaning of life or how to face death. It doesn't matter what I answer. They pay little attention it and instead start thinking about how they would answer their own question. But that's surely the best thing that can happen.

After Vera left, I sent a text to Dorothy.

Thanks for returning to V

She replied a few minutes later.

Couldn't find. Thought you did.

CHAPTER 32

Meg

WHO STOLE VERA'S NECKLACE AND PLANTED IT IN MY ROOM? AND WHO retrieved it from under the plants and put it behind Vera's cushion? The prime candidate for the theft had to be Simon. He was sneaky – I saw him photographing something in the office – and he had the opportunity. He had time to take the pearls and plant them in my room while I was in the park. If it wasn't Simon, then who else had taken a dislike to me?

Was it Miles Reading, wounded by what I said to him; Judy, who I had made fun of; Deidre who clearly thought I was a nuisance; Jim Melling who had been forced to come clean about his cover up? Any of them could have snuck out for a few minutes while everyone was focused on the shocking news about the coronavirus.

Would Josephine Wakefield, incensed by my accusations against Wilde, do the deed? I couldn't imagine that majestic figure sneaking through the corridors. She could have ordered someone to do it.

I had to admit that I had alienated a considerable number of resident in my brief stay. I wasn't shaping up as a great success as an undercover agent.

The question of who retrieved the necklace seemed even more difficult to answer. I could think of only one possibility: Rod Knight. He did the courtyard gardening and was one of the few residents who seemed to like me. Did he find the necklace while weeding? To avoid a fuss, he might have placed the pearls in Vera's seat.

My frayed thoughts were interrupted by a loud knock.

'Who is it?' But before I could get to my feet, Simon Long jerked it open and stepped into my room.

'I need to talk to you, lady.' His jaw was clenched and his fists were balled. I quickly retreated behind an armchair.

'How rude. I didn't invite you in.' My hands gripped the back of the chair.

'I'll say what I have to say and then I'll leave.' He had adopted the tone of someone who assumes he has the upper hand. 'You're up to something. I don't know what it is, but you're getting in the way of what I have to do.'

'What is that?'

'None of your business. I strongly suggest you forget you saw me in the office and this little discussion. Mind your own business and stay out of my way.' He brought his fist down hard on my tea table.

I almost laughed. His scowl, tough words and exaggerated gesture was too melodramatic to be taken seriously. It was a performance, designed to scare little old ladies. I wasn't afraid of him. It was time to mount my ethical high horse.

'You were sneaking around in the office. You were surely trespassing. I'm afraid I will have to tell Sylvie or even the police unless you can justify what you were doing.'

'You wouldn't dare.'

'What are you going to do if I did? Murder me? Abduct me?'

He frowned, as if considering the options. Then he changed tactics. Persuasion.

'Look, I'm not doing anything wrong. I'm acting for the good of Sunnyvale and Mrs Wakefield. Just let me be.'

I stood up straight and adopted my schoolmistress manner. 'I'm afraid I can't accept your assurances without further information.'

Some men, perhaps because of their school experiences, are inclined to give way to authority. We glared at each other. I had more experience, I could see that his resolve was weakening.

'If I tell you, then you'll tell that gaggle of gossips who meet in the café. The whole place will know. Women can't keep anything to themselves.'

I crossed my arms. 'I'm used to keeping confidences. My job required it.' I pointed to the chair that Vera had recently occupied. 'Why don't you sit down?'

He sat with a sigh. 'OK. I'll have to trust you. I'm here on business. I've been hired by a lawyer looking after Mrs Wakefield's affairs to find out if she's being ripped off by her staff.'

'Doesn't her charity work go through a foundation.'

'Yes, that's true. But she insists on having a discretionary fund that she administers herself. A stupid arrangement. How can a decrepit old woman of almost a hundred manage such a large amount of money? But there it is. Anyway, Sunnyvale seems to be her favourite project and a lot of money from that fund has always gone into the place. Lately a fair whack is going astray. The old crone refuses to account for it. She says it's used for necessary expenses. When anyone tries to question her, she insists it's her business and gets cross. And when she gets angry there's no reasoning with her.'

'Have you discovered anything?'

'Something that looks like fraud. Money from her fund is going into Sunnyvale as usual, and then some of it is going out for something called "security" or "promotion". But there are no proper records. We suspect someone is skimming it off.'

I was careful to look suitably astonished and impressed. Now that Long had been persuaded to talk to me, he was clearly enjoying his role.

'I'll tell you one interesting thing,' he said. 'That bitch Deidre Barr drives a Porsche and she has a nice new flat in South Melbourne. All supposedly on her salary.'

'You suspect money's going to her. Why?'

'There are probably others involved. I suspect a man called Harry Staples, who also works here. I think that the Mrs Wakefield has gone senile and these people have learned how to get what they want out of her. My boss wants to start exercising power of attorney over her finances and I'm here to look for evidence.'

I told him about Martin Wilde.

'That's interesting. If he's getting money from residents, I wonder where it's going.'

'Into his own pocket, presumably, or perhaps he and Deidre are working together. She boasted about knowing everything that happens at Sunnyvale.'

'Yes, that would make sense.' Long brooded then suddenly turned on me.

'Don't go blabbing about this to your friends.'

He had adopted the menacing tone again. It was wasted on me.

'I want guilty people to be brought to justice and I have no intention of getting in the way of you achieving that result.'

He broke eye contact and stood. He glanced at my bedside table. 'You got one of these too.'

Judy had left a new document with the usual list of weekly activities. I hadn't read it. I picked up the paper: an invitation to donate money to the Josephine Wakefield Centre for Geriatric Research.

'The old girl's made some bad investments,' said Long. 'Lost a lot of money. To save her dream project she's gone begging to her friends in the high end of town.' He pointed at the document with the dove logo. 'Why not tap the rich patrons at Sunnydale as well?' They might have an interest.'

'In geriatric research? Bit late for that.' I said. 'By the way, did you take Vera's pearl necklace and hide it in my room?'

He looked at me as if I had gone crazy. 'Of course not. Don't start accusing me of every bad thing that happens around here.' He walked out leaving the door open.

He could be lying; private investigators worked in the shadows. But I believed what he said about the Wakefield finances. It fitted my suspicions about Deidre. It explained why she refused to take my accusations about Wilde seriously. Perhaps Jenny had learned something from her aunt about the way she was being exploited. Was she aware Wilde's activities and tried to tell Sara? Maybe Deidre tried to cover their tracks by imprisoning Jenny upstairs and frightening Sara.

It would be easy for someone who had control over Sunnyvale to silence residents. Jenny had been heavily drugged. Was she really senile, or did Deidre want to prevent Jenny from talking?

I had some sympathy for Josephine Wakefield. The people she trusted were stealing from her. They had taken over the institution she was so proud of and were using it for their purposes. And her adopted daughter was being mistreated by them. All she had left to her was her residence and her imperious manner. To add to her woes, she had lost a lot of the money that was supposed to go to the project that was meant to be her legacy.

I shook myself. I had to consider the possibility that Wilde was merely here to help the residents, as Sylvie believed. Robert Knowles told us that he had done a lot of good for people before he became greedy. Maybe he had mended his ways. Maybe I was unjustly suspecting an innocent man. But I didn't like the look of him. I found his manner creepy. It was difficult to believe he was a reformed man. If his objective was to extract money from vulnerable people, Deidre would be an obvious partner in crime.

One thing was clear. Deidre was responsible for Vera's necklace being in my room. She was disappointed when the pearls weren't found. My accusations about Wilde had forced her to act; Deidre had to discredit me and force me to leave Sunnyvale under a cloud. She had to make sure that nothing I said would be believed.

I shivered. Now that she had failed, what would she do next?

It was unlikely that Deidre had planted Vera's necklace in my room. She acted like she knew that I had the necklace, but didn't know where. There was an obvious collaborator. Judy had been flitting in and out of the common room during the news broadcast. She had access to all rooms – and knew where valuables were kept. Judy had encouraged Vera to believe I was the thief.

I decided to confront Judy. She would be in the kitchen or setting out plates and cutlery for lunch.

CHAPTER 33

Meg

I FOUND JUDY IN THE DINING ROOM. THE PLATES IN HER HANDS WOBBLED when she saw me. She put them carefully down on a table, backed away and would have fled if I had not been in the doorway.

'Do you want anything, Mrs Thorne?'

I gestured towards a chair. 'Could we sit and have a talk? It won't take long.'

Reluctantly, she complied. I decided that a direct approach would be most effective.

'You took Vera Chapman's necklace from her room and hid it in mine. Why?'

She jerked away from me. 'I never did, Mrs Thorne.' Her indignation was laid on thick.

I looked at her expectantly but said nothing. A teacher's tactic. Waiting for a response to an accusation was often the best way to get a confession from a student who had plagiarised an assignment.

She fidgeted, straightening her skirt, patting her hair. Seconds went by. Finally, she spoke. 'It was just a joke. You were so high and mighty, telling us about being responsible. We thought we would have a laugh.'

'Making Vera anxious. Opening me up to an accusation of theft. Is this the way you have a laugh?' I was indignant, but I caught the most important part of her statement. 'You said "we". Who was your accomplice?'

She reddened. 'No, I didn't mean that. I don't know why I said it. It was just me.'

'It was Deidre, wasn't it? She put you up to this.'

She shook her head vigorously. 'No, just me.' She turned towards the door as if expecting someone to rescue her. 'Please, I have to finish setting the tables. It was a joke. I didn't think. I'm sorry.' She wrung her hands, then her whole body stiffened into a posture of resistance.

If I had more charm or cunning, or the powers of the Spanish Inquisition, then perhaps I could have cajoled or forced her into telling the truth. But I knew that I was not going to get anything more from her about Vera's necklace. I changed the topic.

'Did you know Jenny Mueller before she moved upstairs?'

Her body relaxed. 'Mrs Mueller? She was such a nice lady. We used to have these chats when I came to her room. She wasn't all that far gone. She told me about her travels and the work she did in her husband's business. She did the books, you know. She was urging me to finish school and try for university. That's not me. I want to get married and start a family, and a job like this is enough to go on with. But she was nice. Sometimes I ran errands for her and she'd give me a tip.'

'What errands?'

'She'd send me to the delicatessen over on High Street to get Turkish delight or a rum baba. I love rum babas too. She always gave me money to get one for myself.' She sighed. 'It's a pity what happened to her. They say it was a stroke. She was perfectly all right one day and the next she had to be taken upstairs. I was supposed to do an errand for her, but there was no time.'

'Do you remember the task?'

'I don't know. She told me she had to do something first, but I was to come to her room after tea. But she was taken away before I arrived.'

'Did you notice anything different about her before she was taken upstairs?'

'Well, she wasn't as lively as usual. She was anxious, as if she had something on her mind. She once told me she had to leave. But now I think that was just the stroke coming on.'

Deidre appeared in the doorway and Judy snapped to attention. 'I have to get this job done.' She started banging plates down on the table to make up for lost time.

Deidre stopped me at the doorway. 'You may be interested to know what happened to that maintenance woman who *fixed* the light in your room. We had to let her go. She seemed more interested in talking to residents than doing her job.'

She smiled in triumph and walked away.

CHAPTER 34

Meg

I FELT ABANDONED. I WAS BY MYSELF, SURROUNDED BY PEOPLE WHO WERE suspicious of me or wished me ill, and Dorothy was no longer around to protect my back. I went my room and rang Lila.

She was troubled and angry. 'They had no valid reason. They just wanted to get rid of her.'

'Deidre is suspicious of me and she suspected that Dorothy was helping. She knows we're connected in some way. She made that obvious.'

'Do you want to get out? Please don't think you have to stay if you don't feel safe.'

A puzzle that we assumed would be simple to solve had led to unexpected complexities and dangers. Something criminal was going on at Sunnyvale and Deidre was probably involved. She couldn't get rid of me with the stolen necklace, but she had removed my protector, Dorothy. What else would she do to stop me causing her trouble? I had good reason for leaving.

But then I thought of Sara Brighouse – so troubled and fearful, not daring to leave her room. I hadn't done enough to help her. I'd probably made things worse.

'No. I can't leave now.'

'You can always contact me. We must talk every day. Let's say that if I don't hear from you at least once every 24 hours, we'll take action.'

'What do you have in mind?'

'We'll do something. Don't worry. They can't keep you there against your will.'

A picture went through my mind of Jenny, pale and drugged, locked in an upstairs ward. But she was supposedly senile and maybe she'd really had a stroke, as Judy said.

'Yes, that's true. I can leave. But not yet. I want to help Sara.'

I needed to tell Lila about the everything I had learned in the past 24 hours. But it suddenly occurred to me that talking in my room could be dangerous. Simon believed that Deidre and perhaps other staff at Sunnyvale were involved in illegal activity. They would want to protect themselves. Had they planted listening devices?. I hadn't noticed any, but I didn't know what to look for.

I moved to the alcove opposite my room. I felt carefully under the chair. I looked up and down the corridor. I was alone. I felt safe to talk.

Lila agreed that Deidre was most likely to be responsible for the attempt to frame me for theft. 'Judy sounds like she's easy to influence, especially by a person in authority.'

'But why is Deidre so suspicious of me? What did she think Dorothy and I were doing together?'

'Perhaps it has something to do with what Simon is uncovering about the financial affairs of Sunnyvale. Maybe she realises she's being investigated and thinks you and Dorothy are involved.'

'Or she suspected Dorothy of helping me when she went to search my room for the necklace and couldn't find it.'

'By the way,' Lila said. 'I discovered something new about Colin Mueller. He made a statement to the Royal Commission on Aged Care. He complained about the way his mother is being treated. He said she is heavily drugged and not properly cared for. He even blamed Mrs Wakefield for cutting costs at the expense of people who most need care. No love lost in that family.'

I reflected that he had reason. The downstairs part of Sunnyvale was run according to the expectations of its upper middle-class residents. It was a different story in the dementia ward upstairs.

I finished the call and noticed Miles Reading was in the neighbouring alcove with a newspaper. I hadn't seen him arrive. How much had he heard? Hopefully nothing, if he was hard of hearing like most of us. What could he make of it anyway and why should he care?

I nodded to him and made my way to lunch.

CHAPTER 35

Meg

I WAS WOKEN FROM A NAP BY A SOFT RUSTLE AT THE DOOR. SARA TOOK MY arm as soon as I opened it.

'Come. I have to show you.' She pulled me with her along the corridor.

I had no time to get my walker. The deterioration she had suffered in the last few days was obvious. Her stoop was more pronounced, her face was grey and her step was unsteady. Her fine grey hair had not been combed. Nevertheless, she held me with a tight grip as we stepped into her room. It was in disarray; papers, books and photographs were scattered on the floor.

She sat me in a chair and began sorting through the collection. She grew frustrated and pushed them away.

'I grew up mostly in London but during the War I lived on my uncle's farm near Buckingham. He had dairy cattle and one was named after me, but it looked so much like the others that I couldn't tell it apart.' She trailed off and shook her head. 'No not that.' It was as if her memories had brought her down a corridor to a dead end.

'Jenny is my best friend and one day we went to the Melbourne show and we lost each other while watching the wood chopping competition. I found her...' Again she stopped and shook her head.

'Can I make you a cup of tea?' I stood and reached for a packet on a shelf over the table.

'No not that!' she cried in alarm and indicated another packet nearer the sink.

I boiled the jug and spooned the tea into the pot. 'You don't take milk, do you?'

'No milk, no sugar. I always drink my tea black. Just like my uncle. He had a small dairy farm near Buckingham. He had about twenty cows and one was named after me.'

She stopped again and then she brightened as if something had just occurred to her. But it took her a long time to get settled on her chair. Finally, she began.

'Once upon a time there was a man and his child, a girl, who lived in a small village. The child's mother had disappeared and the man married another woman, who took them to live in her house made of gingerbread. She was really a witch but for a long time she was a good mother to the girl. The girl was allowed to go almost anywhere in her stepmother's house but one room was forbidden. One day, the girl found the room unlocked and decided to explore it. The ghost of her mother arose from the floor and told her that the witch had killed her and chopped her up. The girl saw blood all over the floor and she ran screaming from the room. One day, she heard her stepmother weeping in her room. She went in, put her arms around her stepmother and heard her confession. But instead of going with her to the magistrate to admit her crime, the witch locked her stepdaughter in the attic where she stayed for the rest of her life.'

A sad story, I thought, but realistic. If a person was capable of murder she would be also capable of doing what needed to be done to cover it up.

Sara told the story without expression. It was as if she had learnt it by heart. Jenny had said that she was trying to make Sara remember something. Was it this strange story that she tried to impress on her memory?

'Did Jenny tell you that story?' I asked.

Sara shook her head. 'No more,' she said, exhausted, and tried in vain to get to her feet.

I helped her to the bed.

'I'll let you rest and come back later.'

She pointed to the large canister of tea on the bookshelf. 'Take it.'

'Thank you but I have plenty of tea.' It wasn't my brand.

'No, you must take it.' Her agitation returned and she tried to get up.

To calm her, I picked up the canister from the shelf and took it with me.

CHAPTER 36

Meg

I sat on my bed and puzzled over what Sara had told me. She had wanted to tell me something but her memory had deteriorated. Her mind kept straying into stories of her childhood or her early days in Australia and the friendship with Jenny.

The story she'd told was about a murder and an imprisonment. Was it the story of the murder of Jenny's mother? I imagined Jenny in her last hours, when she knew she was going to be sent upstairs, trying to impress what she knew about the murder on Sara's memory, so there was a chance that the truth would be revealed. If that was so, had Sara got the account mixed up with memories of her childhood.

Or perhaps Jenny had used the form of a story so that it would be easier for her to remember. How best can you impress a memory on someone who is losing that capacity? But did the story make sense? Her mother had been murdered, but not, according to police investigations, by a wicked stepmother. No one at the time considered Josephine Wakefield was guilty. And if Jenny knew something about the murder why didn't she reveal it earlier?

If Jenny didn't like the aunt who became her adopted mother – and I could understand life under the control of that autocratic woman would be difficult – then perhaps, declining into senility, she came to believe that Josephine had murdered her mother. Or perhaps she did know something about the murder but the memory had been repressed until she came to Sunnyvale and began sharing childhood experiences with Sara.

I didn't know what to think. I needed expert advice.

I found Rod Knight in one of the alcoves near his room. His large frame was hunched over a picture in his hands.

'A family photo,' he said when I announced my presence. 'My sons when they were young. But I can't see their faces anymore.'

I sat beside him and described the features of the two boys in the picture. Rod smiled.

'Yes, that one's Mike,' he said. 'The other one's Sam.'

I told him I was reading a book about repressed memory and wanted his opinion. He looked up, pleased to be diverted onto a subject related to his expertise.

Many experts, he told me, have become sceptical about the existence of repressed memory. Too many cases have turned out to be bogus.

'It's all too easy for people to acquire false memories,' he said. His own opinion was that memories of traumatic events in most cases are not repressed. 'People can remember, but choose not to. They develop ways of preventing themselves from thinking about events in that period of their lives. But if they are forced for some reason to remember, they can. And when they do, what they recall is usually vivid and accurate.'

'If a person is suffering from dementia, is she more likely to let her guard down and remember what she didn't want to remember?'

'Perhaps, though you have to allow that people suffering from dementia, at least in the later stages, are also subject to delusions.' He looked at me kindly. 'I hope you're not worried about yourself.'

'Oh, no. My interest is purely intellectual.' I thanked Rod and left him with his picture.

It seemed to me that either of my ideas could be true. Sara could have brought to the surface memories that she had earlier tried to forget; or she could be delusional. Was it even worth trying to figure out what Sara's story really meant?

When Sara came to my room, she had wanted to show me something. She had been looking through piles of pictures and papers in her room. Perhaps something among these documents might help solve the mystery. When I was able to visit her again, I would help her sort through them.

I was too agitated to sleep, so I went through notes about Elizabeth's death. It wasn't murder. Jenny had the gun, but police believed it was an accidental discharge. Still, I was curious about the other people who might have had cause to be angry with Elizabeth.

Robert and Josephine Wakefield were first on the list. They had a strong motive for wanting to prevent Elizabeth from marrying. That would have cost them half their business and wealth. They had alibis. Would they stand up to a rigorous examination?

Next on the list was Elizabeth's lover. The police decided Leo wasn't a suspect. But why? Were their reasons good enough?

Lila had told me about a few other suspects. A former friend who everyone said had become an enemy, and a disgruntled servant. I could ask Lila to find more information, but the important thing was to talk to Sara and try to clarify what Jenny had told her.

That would have to wait till morning. I climbed back into bed and managed a few hours of fitful sleep.

CHAPTER 37

Jenny

SHE IS AWAKENED BY A CRY. TRAMPING NOISES PASS HER DOOR, VOICES CALL out. Something large is being wheeled along the corridor. The voices fade away, a distant door shuts. She is suddenly afraid.

Sara is looking out for her. She sent someone to see her. Jenny is comforted by this thought and closes her eyes.

She and Sara are eating cheese, bread and blueberries on a grassy knoll near the entrance of a farmhouse. The sign on the gate says, Blueberry Hill Farm. A grassy meadow spreads in front of them to a small bay.

'A perfect day,' says Sara. 'We must have a picture.' She asks a passer-by to help and they have their arms around each other when the picture is taken.

She wakes smiling with the memory. The door opens and Nancy rushes in looking tired and dishevelled.

'I'm sorry I'm late with your breakfast. Someone was brought up here last night and it took time to get her settled. And then there are all the restrictions we need to obey to protect people from the virus. We're a bit late with everything this morning.'

She puts the tray on Jenny's table and opens the blinds.

Jenny has a bad feeling in the pit of her stomach. 'Who was it?'

Nancy hesitates.

'Who was brought up here last night?'

'Sara Brighouse. She had a bad turn.'

'She's my friend. I need to see her.'

'I'm afraid that's impossible. There's the virus; they think she might have it, and anyway she's in a bad state. She's being sedated and is not able to see anyone for the time being. Even her family.'

Nancy rushes off and Jenny sits frozen, any thought of eating breakfast abandoned. She bows her head and the tears spill down her cheeks and onto the bedclothes.

How can I find Sara. Who can help me now?

CHAPTER 38

Meg

I WAS AWAKENED BY UNUSUAL ACTIVITY IN THE CORRIDOR. DEIDRE WAS giving orders and a man replying. I dressed quickly and stepped out of my room. Judy almost fell into my arms.

'Oh, it's so sad. Sara had to be taken upstairs.'

I started towards her door, catching a glimpse of a man from the maintenance staff packing her possessions in boxes. He was wearing a mask and gloves. Deidre blocked me. 'Keep out. Go to your room.'

I dragged Judy with me by the arm. I wanted an explanation. She collapsed into the seat near my bed.

'She became ill during the night and they think she might have this virus.' Judy was close to tears. 'They had to take her away. I brought her food yesterday evening. Do you think I might have it too?' Her eyes widened. I had been in close contact with Sara. Judy jumped from the chair and moved away from me.

It didn't sound logical to me. How could Sara contract Covid-19 in a room by herself? Judy had contact with people outside the home, but she was okay. We looked at each other warily as she backed out the door.

Most residents appeared to be avoiding the common room. Georgia and Wanda were sitting at the back whispering to each other as if preparing for a funeral.

'Of course, it might not be the virus,' said Wanda. 'They say she has a weak heart. It could have been a heart attack. Or maybe her dementia became much worse. She was pretty far gone already.'

I realised they knew no more than me about what happened to Sara. Not wanting to join in fruitless speculation, I returned to my room. Sara's room had been emptied and a man wearing a mask was spraying the floor and furniture. The boxes with her papers and photographs must have been moved to the storeroom.

It had taken little time to erase all traces of her presence.

I sat on my bed in a despondent mood. I was sorry for Sara. Even if she recovered it was unlikely she would ever return to her room. Her dementia had become noticeably worse during my stay. She would remain upstairs.

Her removal also meant that our investigation had come to an end. She was beyond reach physically as well as mentally. We would never know what had frightened her now. We would never know what Jenny wanted her to remember.

A horrible thought occurred to me. Was Sara really ill, or had she been taken upstairs to prevent her from revealing Jenny's secret?

Whoever was trying to frighten her – Deidre was now my prime suspect –might have decided their technique wasn't effective. Better to ensure that Sara couldn't communicate with anyone, especially me. The pandemic provided a handy excuse to remove her quickly without questions being asked. Even her son wouldn't be able to intervene. Upstairs she would be at the mercy of her persecutor. Like Jenny, she could be kept on drugs until her deterioration made that unnecessary. And if she died – perhaps with a little help from Deidre – would anyone pay much attention during a pandemic? I thought of all those corpses piled up around hospitals in Italy, America and the UK. Who had time for a thorough investigation of every death?

I felt powerless as I paced my room. I regret becoming involved in this investigation. I should have stayed in my comfortable little flat. I hadn't been able to do any good, and I had been a cause of the harm that Sara was now suffering. If I hadn't been so eager to talk to her, she probably wouldn't be upstairs now at the mercy of Deidre. Everything I had done had been futile. Every move I made brought Sara closer to the fate everyone here feared.

Was I being too harsh on myself? I merely tried to talk to her. I acted in ignorance and whatever was going on at Sunnyvale has nothing to do with me. But, by undertaking our investigation, we had assumed a responsibility. I had stirred things up when I talked to Sara and by visiting Jenny. I couldn't pretend that I had nothing to do with Sara's removal. I should have known that it could happen. I couldn't plead innocence. And even if I were innocent, I had reason to be concerned about what her welfare. That was a part of the responsibility we accepted when we agreed to find out what was frightening her. And by agreeing to become a resident of Sunnyvale the responsibility devolved mainly on me. I thought of ringing Lila and talking to her about it. But what difference would that make? If anyone was going to act it had to be me.

I stood by the window staring out into the courtyard. You can't be blamed for doing nothing if there is nothing that you can do. I couldn't storm upstairs and rescue Sara by force. I could appeal to her son, but I suspected he would accept the decision of the institution he trusted to care for her.

My job had finished. I could look forward to leaving Sunnyvale.

Then I remembered the pictures and papers that overflowed on Sara's table. They were now in the basement with the rest of her belongings. There was something among them that she wanted to show me. If I could search through them, would there be some clue to explain her fear? It might enable me to help her. That meant getting access to the storeroom.

It was a foolish idea. I would have to sneak into the store room — if it was unlocked — and open Sara's sealed boxes. What if Deidre caught me? The manager said she had an eye on everything that happened at Sunnyvale. I shivered. I should wait until Mr Brighouse claimed Sara's possessions and then ask his permission. But if there was any chance of helping Sara, I had to act now. Deidre might even search Sara's belonging to check for incriminating evidence.

I took a deep breath. Raiding a private storeroom was a new experience — what did I need? Slippers. They wouldn't make any noise when I passed reception. Something sharp. It would open the boxes. A bag. I might need to carry important stuff back to my room. Gloves and a scarf. Just in case Sara did have the coronavirus. Glasses. I had to be able to read any letters.

My kit was swiftly assembled and I cautiously opened the door. The corridor was empty, same with the common room. It seemed that everyone had decided avoiding crowds was the best way to stay healthy. Sylvie wasn't in reception and there was no sign of Deidre. I breathed easier until I saw Miles approaching. We acknowledged each other with a nod, as we were now in the habit of doing.

I pressed the lift button and waited impatiently for the doors to open. No staff or residents were in the basement and I hurried past the empty gym to the storeroom. I turned the handle half expecting, half hoping, it to be locked. It opened silently and the light was still on. The removalist was either careless or lazy.

Sara's possessions were a metre inside the door. Some were easy to move, probably clothes. I pushed them away and came to a heavy box. The tape was swiftly sliced and I scooped out dozens of letters. At first, I thought that they might contain a clue. Perhaps Sara had written to someone about her fears, or what Jenny had told her. But I soon found they were dated from many years ago. I pushed them aside and dug out some photos. Most were old. A man in a suit and a woman in a long dress posed formally, possibly Sara's parents or the Buckingham uncle and aunt. There was a baby on a rug, a toddler with a toy truck. Most likely they were Sara's son.

The next pictures were scenes in Australia. Jenny was in many, sometimes with a man. I presumed he must have been her husband. Then my eyes fastened on a photo of Sara and Jenny. It was a close up. They were older, late middle age, I thought. They were laughing, embracing. Behind them was a sign: Blueberry Hill Farm.

The same name as the song that triggered Sara's fear at the recital. It was another piece of the puzzle – but where did it fit? The photo indicated a happy occasion for the friends. Hearing the song had made Sara afraid. Had someone used the song to trigger that fear, or was it a coincidence? I suspected Deidre was sending a message to Sara: Jenny would be harmed if she revealed her secret.

I returned the photos to the box. Whatever Jenny and Sara shared, I decided, had little to do with events that happened sixty years ago. What was important to them was a deep and abiding friendship. I remembered the look on Sara's face when she heard the song that reminded her of being with Jenny: sadness, longing.

My thoughts were interrupted by a heavy footsteps on the stairs. There was a grunt; Deidre was on her way. It was too late reach the lift or hide in the gym. I hastily rearranged the boxes and looked for a place to hide. There was nothing to shield me, I would be caught immediately if Deidre entered the storeroom. A man's voice called out and Deidre stopped. There was a loud sigh, the footsteps retreated. The man called again. It was Miles; he urgently wanted Deidre. There was a brief argument at the head of the stairs and then I heard feet clumping on the corridor above.

I was shaking as I rose to my feet and almost forgot my walker. I turned off the light, closed the door, and shuffled to the lift. No one was in the corridor or the office. I made it to lounge and collapsed into a chair in the corner.

Miles appeared a few minutes later and sat on the sofa opposite. He had a newspaper and scrutinised the front page as if he were committing it to memory. Deidre looked in and glared at us.

'Nothing really wrong,' she told Miles. 'You both should be in your rooms.'

He put down the paper. 'I was having trouble flushing my toilet. Too bad she got rid of that handywoman.' He winked.

Miles had saved me from Deidre. I realised it wasn't the first time. It was Miles who had retrieved the pearl necklace from the garden. He was in the corridor when the search party set out for my room. He must have seen me slip the necklace out the window. He knew how to discreetly return it to Vera.

I leaned forward. 'Thank you.'

He looked at me for a long time, then put out his hands to take mine. He stopped half way, as if remembering the new rule about close contacts. I took his hands and squeezed them. Social distancing be damned.

CHAPTER 39

Meg

WITH A SHAKY HAND I MADE MYSELF A CUP OF TEA AND REVIEWED WHAT I had learned from my perilous visit to the storeroom. I understood why the Blueberry Hill song made such an impression on Sara, but I had made no progress in solving the mystery that involved Jenny. I had found nothing that connected Sara's fear or her story of the witch to fraudulent activities at Sunnyvale Home – if there was a connection. I believed that Deidre was responsible for frightening Sara, but I had no proof.

I wandered around the room with cup in hand, trying to think if I had missed anything. My eyes fell on the tea canister that Sara insisted I take. It had been important, but Sara couldn't tell me why.

I took the container to the bathroom sink and, using a cup, I ladled the leaves carefully into a bowl, running my finger through each scoop. At the bottom was a thick envelope. it was addressed in a scrawled but clear hand to Mr Colin Mueller. A letter from Jenny to her son. This was the errand she wanted Judy to do for her: to post this letter. But for some reason, Jenny hid it inside the canister and gave it to Sara.

I brushed off the dust and put the letter on my bed. I was tempted to tear it open and read what Jenny had to say. But opening it would be wrong. Jenny meant it for her son. He would know best what to do with whatever it contained. My duty was to ensure he received it.

The letter had no stamp. Judy was probably expected to take care of that. The problem was easily solved. I always carry a few stamps in my handbag. I would take this letter out and post it. Then I would tell Lila and Dorothy my suspicions about what happened to Sara. They would inform Mr Brighouse and his lawyer, and they could work out the best way to rescue Sara. My job was almost done. I was eager to leave Sunnyvale and go home.

With a lighter heart I put on my overcoat, put the letter the inside pocket and shuffled down the corridor to the front door. But when I punched in the code, the door refused to budge. I tried again with no success.

'I'm sorry,' Sylvie was behind me. 'We're in lockdown.'

'Why?'

'It's to protect residents from the virus,' Sylvie said. 'No visitors can come in and only staff can go out. Anyway, there's no point going out. All the businesses around here are shut by order of the state government.'

Deidre suddenly appeared. With her was the burly male nurse I saw upstairs.

'Come Mrs Thorne, you are supposed to be in your room. We have a case of Covid-19 in the building and we must take precautions. No more gathering in public spaces. All meals will be served in your room.'

They herded me back to my room, staying a few steps behind. I had the impression that they would have used a cattle prod if they had one. They waited until I was inside my room and then shut the door behind me.

When they had gone, I tried the door. It was locked.

I needed to contact Lila. I opened the drawer in the bedside table where I had left my mobile phone. It wasn't there. I felt in all corners of the drawer. Nothing. With a rising sense of panic, I went through the drawers in the wardrobe, checked under the chair cushions and searched the bookshelf, though I had no reason to believe it could be in any of those places. Someone had taken it from my room.

They would have had plenty of opportunity. Once Dorothy had been evicted from Sunnyvale I had gone back to my old habit of leaving my phone behind. If you don't carry a handbag and have no pockets, it's merely an inconvenience.

I turned to the red phone on the table near my bed. I had never used it, but now was the time. I picked it up and it began buzzing.

Sylvie finally answered. 'I'm sorry Mrs Thorne, but I've been instructed not to allow you to make a call at this time. Your friend can't come to see you. We're in lockdown.' She was talking to me as if I were hysterical. Perhaps I sounded that way.

'Please, Mrs Thorne, you need to calm down. I suggest you lie down and relax. Don't worry. You'll be well looked after.'

'Please, could you give me Miles Reading's number?'

'He's not allowed to visit you. Please, Mrs Thorne. Be calm and lie down. If you really need someone, press the buzzer and a nurse will come.'

She hung up.

I was trapped. I turned on my television, not knowing what else to do. A picture appeared of an elderly patient on a ventilator. Medical staff covered almost entirely in white gowns and hoods, their faces protected by masks, monitored the screen near the bed.

The scene changed to a supermarket where shoppers were fighting over toilet paper. A cruise ship appeared on the screen. A reporter standing in front of a harbour background told us that more and more passengers were becoming ill with the coronavirus. A man and woman aboard the ship appeared on the screen pleading to be rescued.

Lila had compared my visit to Sunnyvale to a voyage on a cruise ship. The analogy had taken on a sinister connotation.

I switched off the television and paced my room, trying to work out what to do. The letter lay on my bed. Perhaps I should try to get Judy to send it. But I suspected that any attempt I made to contact the outside world would be thwarted. It was not just the virus. Someone wanted to keep me locked up and isolated and the pandemic simply made that easier. I was sure that was Deidre. She had stolen my phone and told the staff to prevent me making calls. She was involved in a racket, probably with Martin Wilde. She was undoubtedly responsible for moving Jenny upstairs and she had just got rid of Sara in the same way.

I looked at the letter again. The reason for not reading it no longer applied. I couldn't get it to Colin Mueller, at least not right away. If I knew the contents, there was some chance I could pass Jenny's message to someone else, even if I could never send the letter.

I prised it open and found sheets of thin paper covered on both sides by handwriting, cramped but perfectly legible.

CHAPTER 40

Jenny

HARRY HAS GIVEN HER AN INJECTION, BUT THIS TIME SHE FIGHTS AGAINST ITS effects, shaking her head and tossing from side to side to stay awake. She is losing consciousness, floating in a void and a force is pulling her downward into darkness. Jenny knows she must struggle against the black tide that is carrying her away. She is drowning, but then its power wanes and she is aware of light and a noise.

She concentrates on that sound; a steady thumping. Like a heart, or someone beating a carpet. Or is it something more sinister? She doesn't want to think about that.

My name is Jenny Mueller. My friend Sara is in trouble. I must find her.

Surrounding her is a swirling mist and she can't move. She weeps with frustration.

When she comes up again from the darkness her mind is clearer. She hears voices coming from above her.

'She's very restless this morning. She's been like that since I told her about the new patient in my ward.'

'That was a mistake.' The voice is cold.

Jenny knows who this cold person is, and she doesn't want her near. She shuts her eyes tight and turns away.

'They always get upset when something like that happens, and in this case she knows the woman.'

'Shall I get Harry to give her another injection?'

Jenny is afraid and lies still.

'No, she's calmer now, but keep an eye on her.' The voices go away.

I am Jenny Mueller.

She needs to do something. But what she must do is fading from her mind. Only the sense of urgency remains. She tries to sit up but her limbs won't obey. She lies back and floats once again in a fog.

She is outside with Rosie in the park near her mother's flat. It's a beautiful spring day. They are sitting on a bench watching children in the playground. It seems no different from all the other times they have visited, but Jenny is looking down at Rosie and her young self from what seems to be a vast distance. She knows that something bad is going to happen. She wants to call out a warning, but it's like watching a movie. You know that a person is in danger, but there is nothing you can do.

'I have to get something at the milk bar,' says Rosie. 'Wait here until I get back.' She has taken up smoking and probably wants a pack of cigarettes.

Young Jenny waits, humming to herself, watching the children. The wind is changing, and clouds suddenly hide the sun. Rosie is taking a long time and little Jenny is getting cold. She stands up shivering, walks once around the playground, and then decides to go home. Rosie will guess she is there. It's not far.

She makes her way across the park, up a street, and climbs the stairs to the main entrance to her mother's block of flats. Opposite the door is a desk and behind is the cabinet that contains mail and messages for residents. No one is there. Jenny makes her way up the wide wooden stairway to the second floor flat. The door is locked, but Jenny knows where the key is hidden and she takes it from under the mat.

Before she can put it in the door, she hears a loud popping noise, like someone has just opened a bottle of champagne. She hesitates, looks through the keyhole, but sees only an empty hallway.

As soon as she enters the hallway she knows that something is wrong. There is a strange unpleasant smell in the air. She hears a noise and calls out.

'Mother?'

Then she hears a rasping, choking sound coming from the lounge. Someone is attacking her mother, she thinks, and remembers that there is a gun in the drawer of her mother's desk. 'Don't be afraid to use it if necessary,' her mother has told her.

The study is across the hall. She tiptoes across, then strides through the room and opens the drawer. The gun isn't there. She runs her fingers along the side and back. It's empty.

She hears another noise and hesitates. Someone is moving through the dining room into the kitchen.

'Mother?' she says again, this time louder.

The door to the kitchen is open. Jenny reaches in time to see someone leaving the flat by the back entrance. It is dark in that corner and the figure is a grey shape in a large cloak. A sleeve catches between door and the frame. She sees that it is a stained red, with a button on the cuff. The door opens slightly, the sleeve scrapes through, losing its button, and then the door slams shut.

Jenny hears footsteps racing down the stairs. A car starts and drives away.

She goes to the back door and cautiously opens it. No one is on the stairs and the street is empty. She sees the button and stoops to pick it up. Where has she seen it before? She puts it in her pocket.

Jenny knows that she has to search for her mother and she is afraid. She returns through the dining room into the hallway.

The door to the lounge is closed, there's no sound of her mother. She turns the handle.

'Mother!' she says and forces herself to look inside.

'Mother!' Jenny is sitting up in bed at Sunnyvale, her heart beating fast, as she tries to shake the memory out of her head. It won't budge. It's the one memory that she most wants to forget.

'Mother.' It's barely a whisper. She pushes the door wide open; she is too late. The bad thing has happened.

Jenny sees her mother's shoes first and then her legs. Her mother is lying on her back on the carpet, her white blouse is covered in blood. The gun is beside her on the carpet.

Jenny picks it up runs to the kitchen. She's ready to use it even though the intruder is long gone. She dashes down the back stairs, hurtles across the street without looking for traffic, and into the park.

Rosie grabs her arm and brings her to a halt. 'Where have you been? What's happened?'

'My mother...' Jenny gasps but can't say any more. Then Rosie sees the gun and takes it from her hand.

'Tell me, what did you do?'

But Jenny can't talk. There are no words for what she has experienced.

Rosie draws her tightly against her chest. 'What did you see?'

She can't see Rosie's face but Jenny can tell that she is scared. The memory of the blood stain on her mother's chest makes her legs feel weak. She collapses against Rosie.

'My mother,' she says. 'She's been shot.'

Rosie helps her to a bench, sits her down. 'Did you see anyone?'

Jenny shakes her head.

Rosie lets out a breath. 'Just as well. If he had seen you, he might have killed you too.'

She hadn't thought of that. She starts shaking.

Rosie gathers her up in her arms. 'We'll go to your aunt's place.'

She doesn't want to be with her aunt, but there is nowhere else to go.

When they find her aunt in the kitchen, Rosie speaks. 'Someone shot her mother. An intruder. She didn't see who it was.'

Jenny opens her mouth to tell her aunt that she saw her mother bleeding on the lounge room floor, but no words come. She slumps against Rosie.

'An intruder,' her aunt repeats. 'I'll call the police.'

Jenny opens her mouth again, but her voice chokes and she bursts into tears. Her aunt sits beside her, stroking the back of her head. Celia, her aunt's cook, gives her a cup of tea. Then her aunt gets up and takes Rosie out of the room. The phone rings. Celia leaves the kitchen to answer it.

'Oh, poor Elizabeth! Poor woman!' she exclaims, and she hears Celia's footsteps rushing towards the front of the house to find her aunt.

Jenny huddles on a chair until she hears Celia return with Rosie and her aunt.

'The police will soon be there,' her aunt announces. 'I'll call Robert.' She turns to Jenny 'You'll have to stay here. You'll need your things. I'll get Celia to collect them.'

She is now with her aunt in one of her guest rooms.

'The detectives will want to interview us,' Aunt Josephine says. 'But they won't bother you. We'll tell them you were in the park with Rosie when it happened and she can confirm our statement. Best for you to stay out of their way in your room.'

The doctor has given her a sedative and she can hardly keep her eyes open. Her aunt helps her to get undressed, pulls the blanket over her and gives her a hug. 'You'll be all right. You're safe here.'

'Will I have to go to an orphanage?'

'Don't be silly.' Aunt Josephine gives Jenny another hug and gets up to turn off the light.

Jenny wants to cry, but sleep comes first.

It's late morning when she wakes. Light is coming through the curtains. At first she thinks she is at home in her bed. She is groggy and rubs her eyes to force herself awake.

An image of blood spreading out over her mother's blouse comes to her. She is in her aunt's house and her mother is dead. Perhaps she dreamed it all, she tells herself. Perhaps it didn't really happen. But in the pit of her stomach, she knows better.

She walks to the window to opens the curtains and look down on a group of men huddled in the rain on the footpath. Some have cameras. A police car is parked in the drive.

She puts on the clothes that her aunt gave her to wear and creeps downstairs. The lounge room is closed off and she hears the muffled voices of two men talking. The police, she thinks. She doesn't want them to know that she's there so she tiptoes quietly past the door and heads towards the kitchen. Her aunt and uncle are sitting around the table. There is no sign of their cook. They have their back to her and don't notice her presence.

Her aunt is talking. 'The cook says she found the body when she returned from visiting her family. She didn't see anyone.'

A picture comes into Jenny's mind of a coat sleeve caught in the crack of a door. She stops in the kitchen doorway.

Her uncle makes an impatient gesture. 'It's blindingly obvious. The neighbour said she saw Leo leaving the flat in a hurry just after 2.30. She said they had been yelling at each other.'

'Perhaps she told him she wasn't going to marry him after all.'

'Whatever she said, she made him very angry.'

Jenny pictures the body of her mother lying on the floor.

Suddenly Jenny is sitting in a chair beside her aunt. She must have fainted.

Aunt Josephine has her arm around Jenny's shoulders. 'You should stay in bed,' she says. 'I'll give you another sedative.'

Rosie comes in and her aunt looks at her expectantly.

'I told them I took Jenny to the park after lunch,' says Rosie. 'We were there for almost two hours and then we came here.'

'It's a good thing,' says her uncle, 'that you didn't take her home.'

'I invited them over here for tea and scones,' says her aunt. Rosie looks at her quickly and nods.

Jenny has the impression that her mother has been abandoned on the shore of a desolate island. She wants to stop this happening but there is nothing she can do. She bows her head and bursts into tears.

Her aunt strokes her on the back of her head. 'Don't be sad. Don't worry. I'll look after you.'

The police, when they talk to Jenny, are kind and patient.

'Did you know that your mother kept a revolver in her desk?'

'Yes.'

'Did you know how to use it?'

'My mother taught me.'

'You heard noises in the lounge room, so you took it from the drawer.'

Her memory of what she did is confused. But she thought that must be so. She can sense the cold metal of its handle in her hand.

'You went into the lounge room.

She nods.

'What did you see?'

She tries to picture it, but the scene is a blur. 'There was blood. On her blouse. On the carpet.'

'What did you do with the gun? Did you fire it?'

She shakes her head. But someone did. It went off.

'What did you do with it?'

'I took it away.'

'When you left the apartment, you had it in your hand?'

'Yes. Rosie took it from me.'

After the police leave, she feels sick and stumbles into the kitchen, but before she can get to the sink she almost faints and falls into a chair.

She knows that the police think that she killed her mother, and she feels the metal of the gun in her hand. Yes, it must have been her. She was frightened and she must have pulled the trigger. She leans over the floor and gags.

Sitting up in bed, Jenny tries to picture her mother's face but it is obscured by a mist and all she can see is the blood on her blouse, blood on the carpet, and now blood seems to be spreading out over the floor, reaching the door, washing up against the walls. She breathes deeply, concentrating on the light over her bed, and tries to calm herself by leaning back on her pillow.

But memory draws her back to her aunt's kitchen.

She is holding herself up in a chair, trying to control the sickness. Rosie comes in with a bag of clothes in her hands. She's surprised. Jenny sways and Rosie drops the bundle and rushes to support her as she vomits over the floor. She watches it trickle over the tiles towards the bag that Rosie has dropped, the contents spilled across the floor.

As she recovers, Jenny sees the old grey coat that her aunt uses for the garden. The cuff with its worn lining trails out along the side of the bag. One of the buttons is missing and the torn thread dangles on the floor. On the side of the sleeve is a red stain.

Jenny reaches in her pocket and grasps the button that she picked up at her mother's back door. Her body goes rigid.

Rosie looks down and sees what Jenny is staring at. She lets go of her shoulders and pushes the coat back into the bag.

'It's nothing,' she says. 'Don't worry about it. Your aunt got it dirty when she was gardening. She wants me to take it to the cleaners.'

Jenny continues staring. 'I saw...'

Rosie grabs a rag from the sink, kneels and dabs at the vomit ineffectively. She is crying.

'Your mother,' she says between sobs. 'She knew about us. She said she would go to the police. She said I would go to prison.'

'You?' Jenny whispers. She can barely breath. She pictures Rosie wearing her aunt's coat disappearing around the kitchen door. But she is short and plump. The person who left by the stairs was not Rosie.

'No!' Rosie cries looking up. 'How can you think that? It wasn't me.' She holds her arms wide. Her hands smell of vomit.

Her voice drops to a whisper. 'I didn't ever think...' She swallows and starts again. 'Believe me I wouldn't have...' She pauses again and strokes the side of Jenny's face. Her voice becomes softer and more intimate. 'But she had to be stopped. There would have been a scandal. We only wanted to protect you.'

Jenny wants to push Rosie away but is too weak.

'It's my fault that I left you alone in the park. I was chatting with the girl in the shop. That's all I did. But you shouldn't have gone back there. Why did you?'

Jenny turns away. Rosie pulls her back towards her. 'Don't be difficult. I just want the best for you. Let's imagine we were in the park together all that time. That's the way it was supposed to be. Don't think about what you saw. There's no point in thinking about such things. Nothing you can do will change what happened. Think only of good things. How your aunt and uncle are being kind to you. The nice life you will have with them. Then everything will be all right.'

'And after all,' she says as she straightens, 'you don't want to hurt them. You don't want to hurt me. And no one will believe you.'

When Aunt Josephine returns, her aunt's face has assumed the mournful expression that she will wear for weeks. She glances at the vomit on the floor and at Rosie who is washing out the rag.

'You can go. Celia will clean the floor. And you my poor dear,' she says to Jenny. 'Let's go upstairs. You need a change of clothes. I'll see if there is something for you to wear.'

Jenny lets Aunt Josephine take her arm and help her to her feet. The button falls to the floor.

They both stare at it.

'It's from an old coat,' explains her aunt. 'Nothing you need to worry about.' She picks it up and throws it in the bin under the sink.

'It's gone. Forget about it.'

The door to Jenny's room opens and Nancy appears. It's struggle not to say what she is thinking.

I did not kill my mother. I have always known that. And I have always known who did.

CHAPTER 41

Meg

I LET THE PAGES OF THE LETTER FALL ONTO MY BED. I STOOD AND STARED absently at the wall.

I knew Jenny's secret and I could guess why Sara was so afraid. Jenny had at last remembered what happened on the day her mother died: Josephine Wakefield, was the killer.

Jenny must have confronted Mrs Wakefield. She protected herself by having Jenny taken to the dementia ward where she could be drugged. Any accusations against the Sunnyvale founder would never be believed.

Jenny must have told her best friend what she remembered. But she was frustrated by Sara's mental decline, living mostly in the past. Nevertheless, Jenny was able to get her to remember a fairy tale version of the murder. And Jenny had left her letter to Colin in a canister on Sara's shelf. She would have known was about to be moved upstairs.

Then Josephine had Deidre, or another accomplice, intimidate Sara. Jenny would be hurt if Sara revealed the secret. That was the source of Sara Brighouse's great anxiety.

I felt sorry for Sara and Jenny. Their problems were caused by a selfish woman. The police were fed lies that Jenny had accidentally fired the gun. The therapists Jenny saw in hospital undoubtedly accepted this account without question. They would have concentrated on getting her to overcome her consequent feelings of guilt. Perhaps Jenny even believed that she had done the deed, creating memories of carrying the gun into the lounge room and having it go off in her hand. Then she did her best to forget.

I thought about how much this effort must have cost her; of what a toll it must have taken on her mental health.

Josephine's plan unravelled when Jenny began to remember the truth. It might have been sparked by the reunion of the old friends at Sunnyvale. Clarity could have emerged following Sara's suggestion to write her account of the events. For one reason or another, Jenny was able to remember what happened – just as the psychologist Rod Knight said trauma victims are able to do.

The key, I suspected, was remembering that there was no gun in the drawer. She couldn't have killed her mother. This was what she wanted to tell me when I visited her upstairs. The drawer was empty.

I now knew who killed Elizabeth and why Sara lived in a state of fear. But what was I going to do about it?

I had to get out of my room and find a way of communicating with Lila or Dorothy.

The courtyard was my best hope as there were two doors to the residential wings. If I could get through one of them, I might be able to find someone who would lend me a phone. After that I could escape from Sunnyvale through an emergency door. An alarm would sound. But I might be able to reach the street and flag a motorist before the staff responded.

Or perhaps not. The world was in lockdown. All the assumptions about how to get help in an emergency were no longer reliable.

I sat on my bed, not able to decide what to do. I'm not brave and my natural inclination was to wait for rescue. Lila said she would find a way of helping me if I could not contact her. But she and Dorothy were locked out and I was locked in, and I couldn't help thinking that I was in danger.

I imagined Deidre barging into my room. She would overpower me and force me to go upstairs. Miles couldn't save me again – he was confined to his room. The corridors would be empty. No one would see what was happening. No one would rescue me.

I felt like weeping, but there was no alternative. I had to act.

"What doesn't kill you makes you strong." I have never thought much of Nietzsche as a philosopher. Much of what he said, including this statement, is false. But if you are faced with life threatening peril on one hand and a small possibility of escape on the other, then Nietzsche is the philosopher to go to for inspiration.

I put the letter back in the canister and filled it with the tea. There was no point in trying to sneak it out. If I was caught it would be found. If I left it and managed to escape I would find a way of retrieving it.

Then I turned to the window overlooking the courtyard. It was not meant to be an escape hatch. A metal chain limited the opening to about a foot. However, the designer did not have in mind a small person like me.

I pushed my chair up to the window and forced my body through the gap. It was a tight fit and for a few moments I thought I was stuck. Lila was right; I had gained weight. I drew in my stomach and jerked my body through a few millimetres at a time. With a last strong pull, one arm pressing against the pane, I was released from the window like a cork from a bottle, almost toppling past the garden bed onto the concrete.

I landed on my hands and knees. It took me a moment to catch my breath, then I felt my way gingerly around the succulents and onto the path. I couldn't see any residents or staff as most of the curtains were drawn. I set off for the exit furthest away from reception.

I had used my walker for so long that I'd lost my sense of balance. I kept lurching and had to grab the side of the bird bath, then the back of one of the cast iron chairs, then the table to stay upright. I arrived at the door exhausted and more pessimistic about my chances of escape. The plan of moving quickly around the building into the street was obviously delusional.

I peered around the edge of the exit door and saw no one in the corridor. People were obeying the new rules. Had they been locked away like me?. Georgia was at the other end of the building near reception; I didn't know where Miles lived. I hesitated, then knocked at the nearest door.

To my relief it was opened by Wanda. I stepped towards the threshold and she backed away.

'Wanda, I need help.'

She continued backing away. 'You can't come in, please!' She looked like she would scream if I took another step. She did not see me as the nice old lady with whom she shared a table in the dining room, I must have been the grim reaper with a scythe.

I stopped outside her door. 'Please, I need to contact my friend and I've lost my phone. Could you let me use yours? You can wipe it down with disinfectant afterwards and wash your hands.'

'I'm so sorry, I'm a technophobe.' She grimaced. 'I don't have a mobile phone, computer or one of those pads. Can't you ask at the office?'

I heard footsteps coming down the corridor. More than one person, moving fast. In a moment they would come around the corner and see me.

I turned and headed towards the emergency exit, pushing off against the wall to keep upright.

They caught me before I reached it. A strong arm wrapped around my torso and brought me to a stop.

'Hold her still.' It was Deidre. I tried to push myself away but I was in Harry's strong grip. He breathed heavily onto the back of my neck, smelling of peppermint toothpaste. The side of my face was pressed into his shoulder. I could see a few residents, aroused by the noise in their corridor, poking their heads around their doors.

'Now, now Mrs Thorne, don't be so upset. You're safe with us. We'll protect you from the virus. You don't have to be so afraid. You don't have to run away. There, there. We'll take good care of you and all the other residents.'

While Deidre talked, I saw she was taking a syringe out of a brown medic bag.

'Help,' I gasped and fought desperately but to no avail. Expertly, she gave the needle a squirt and inserted it into my arm.

The light became dim. The grip on me loosened and it seemed that I was falling through the floor, tumbling down into the dark.

CHAPTER 42

Jenny

THE DAY IS FADING THROUGH THE BLINDS. NANCY SERVES DINNER AS SHE always does before ending her shift. She's in a hurry.

'There's a Covid-19 case in the hospital ward.' She pauses as she removes Jenny's tray. 'Don't worry,' she says hastily. 'You're safe. We're keeping the woman isolated.'

Jenny is expecting Harry to come with the evening injection. He's late. She listens to noises in the corridor outside her door.

Where did they put Sara? Is she in a room near me?

She doesn't pay much attention to the television with its flashing pictures and chatter. She prefers silence. Nancy knows this and leaves it off. Sometimes a nursing assistant or a cleaner turns it on while Jenny is dozing. She knows about the pandemic and that it has been lethal for the elderly.

Jenny remembers her mother telling her not to go to the park because of the polio epidemic. She didn't suffer from that disease. Perhaps she will get this one. But she doesn't want to die yet. She needs to find Sara.

She feels the urgency. Sara is here – perhaps not far away – and she might be dying of Covid. If Jenny can find her, then she can put her arms around Sara and lie by her side. Sara will know Jenny is with her. If she has the disease, then at least they will be together.

It's getting dark. No one has come to give her an injection. As she listens to the bustle in the corridor, Jenny realises that everyone is probably too busy. They have forgotten her.

Jenny is wide awake and alert for the first time in many days. She feels strong enough to get out of bed. She has no idea of what will happen if she goes looking for Sara. The nurses might find her, return her to bed and give her the injection. But she must try. This is her only chance.

Jenny is anxious to move. She wants to stride out of the room and find Sara. It's too early. She must wait until the noise subsides and most of the staff have gone home.

She props herself on the pillow and concentrates on staying awake.

CHAPTER 43

Meg

I BECAME AWARE OF A WHITE LUMINESCENCE AND SOMETHING BLINKING beside. Gradually I became aware that I was looking at a ceiling bathed in fluorescent light. I knew I had to get up, but when I found I couldn't move I lost consciousness.

Next time my eyes opened I thought that I was at home. But the bed position was wrong and my arms seemed to be trapped. Something was covering the lower half of my face. Nausea overwhelmed me when I tried to see where I was. I knew I had to get out of bed, I had an urgent task, but I couldn't think what it was. I looked at the ceiling light and fought to stay awake; it wavered, blurred and disappeared.

In the distance I heard the crash of metal, a voice, footsteps. I focused on the sounds; they slowly drew me back to consciousness. I was groggy but able to open my eyes. I was in a narrow room, the door that was closed. A panel of instruments beside me explained the first impression of blinking lights. I tried to turn to but my arms were strapped to the bed.

I panicked, straining against the straps, my body bucking as I fought in vain to free myself. The nausea returned and I lay back exhausted, breathing heavily.

Where was I? I remembered fleeing down the corridor at Sunnyvale; the emergency door in the distance; being gripped by the male nurse; Deidre's needle going into my arm.

They would have taken me away in a stretcher, not to a hospital where I might be able to contact someone, but upstairs, where residents were locked away when they needed special treatment.

I cried out and jerked against the straps. I stopped when I heard footsteps approaching. The door opened a fraction, a face appeared and then vanished. I caught a glimpse of an open space, carts lined up against a wall.

I made myself lie still and think. I must be in the medical wing, away from other residents.. The medical equipment suggested I was being treated for something – but I wasn't attached to any machine.

More footsteps, the door opened to reveal two people, one slender and tall, the other stocky and shorter. They were covered head to foot in white gowns, hoods drawn down to the shields that covered their faces. They reminded me of the medicos on television attending a coronavirus patient. The plastic distorted their faces, they could have been aliens from a space ship. The shorter one approached and bent over – it was Deidre.

'She's awake. Shall I give her another dose?'

The tall person came closer. 'No. It could knock her out for good. We don't want that to happen now.'

It was Josephine Wakefield.

Deidre tugged at the straps. 'Well, she's not going anywhere.'

'Best to wait. When the medical people are overwhelmed with cases we can ship her out then. The other one too. Two deaths in a nursing home won't be surprising. Who will have the time to investigate in a pandemic?'

'Her friend Lila Galli might cause trouble.'

Josephine's gown fluttered with a shrug. 'We are in a state of emergency. People will have to learn to accept the deaths of their friends and loved ones without making a fuss. A feeble woman dying of Covid-19. What's strange about that?'

'Should we fill out a donation form for her. It wouldn't be difficult to forge her signature. It's on the admission form in the office. It's natural that someone so ill might want to give a donation to the institution that cared for her. We can get Harry as a witness.'

'No,' said Josephine. 'It's not worth it in her case. Martin checked her accounts. All she has is a middling amount of money in a superannuation fund. They ask too many questions.'

'What shall we do with her now?'

'Just leave her be. Give her some water. Tell Harry to look in on her from time to time and tell the other staff to stay well away. She's supposed to have the virus, and they won't want to be infected.'

There was no doubt who was in control. Deidre was the one who followed orders. Her gloved hand held a glass to my face and dribbled water into my mouth. Did it contain more drugs? I had no choice because I was so thirsty. I choked, swallowed some more and struggled to speak.

'You won't get away with it.' My croak didn't sound convincing. Neither bothered to respond.

When the door closed behind them, I began to shake with fear. I was trapped, they were going to kill me and there was nothing I or my friends could do about it.

How could a peaceful, tolerant, law abiding retired philosopher come to an end like this? But then I reflected that it was the fate of many elderly people with dementia to end up in a secure wing of a nursing home. I was unusual – I was the victim of homicidal criminals.

I began to slip from consciousness again and didn't try to fight it. What was the point?

CHAPTER 44

Jenny

SHE IS TRYING TO TEACH SARA TO HOW TO SERVE A TENNIS BALL. 'YOU HOLD your racquet like this.' Sara swings and misses the ball. It drops down near her feet. She laughs.

'I'm terribly uncoordinated. I was always bad at sports. Not like you. I can't even swim properly. Don't ask me to go swimming in the ocean. If I'm swept out you'll have to rescue me.'

Jenny wakes with a start. For a moment she can't remember what she is supposed to do. Then it comes to her – she needs to visit Sara. Is it too late? No light is coming through the blinds, there's no noise from the corridor.

For a moment she wonders if she has the strength to stand. It's been so long since she felt the floor. Jenny doesn't feel the same urgency, searching for Sara is an impossible undertaking – unlikely to succeed.

Memories of friendship force her to sit up; Sara needs help. Her feet search in vain for slippers. She leans forward and just saves herself from falling face-first onto the floor.

Easy. No point in trying to hurry.

She straightens and takes baby steps toward the door where her robe hangs. She puts it on, cautiously turns the door handle and peers out.

The corridor is empty. Which way should she go? Footsteps approach from around the corner, Jenny steps back into her room. There is no time to close the door. Harry rushes past without looking her way. He uses a swipe card to enter another corridor.

Her room is surrounded by a dozen more. She opens the first door. 'Sara,' she whispers.

An old man turns toward her, she quickly closes it. The next room is empty. The third holds the sleeping form of a large person wrapped in a quilt.

This is hopeless. I'll never find her.

But she tries another door. The female occupant is blubbering and looks terrified.

'Sorry,' she whispers.

The next room is empty, a man's cough saves her checking the following chamber.

I'll try one more.

There's a motionless form on the bed. The hallway light reveals long grey hair over a white sheet. Jenny's heart skips: Sara.

She closes the door and moves to the bed.

'Sara. It's me, Jenny.'

She touches her friend's shoulder. Sara flinches. 'Sara,' Their faces are almost touching.

It's really her. But what should I do now?

Her drug-free mind knows the answer.

We must get out of this place and find somewhere safe.

She pictures the grassy slope near that farm in Tasmania where they once had a picnic lunch.

She shakes Sara. 'We must go,' Sara groans but doesn't wake.

She's drugged.

Jenny tries to pull Sara into a sitting position, but her friend is heavy and floppy. She rests against the bed, panting.

She can't rescue Sara – but she won't desert her. Jenny removes the robe and makes space in the bed. She wraps her arms around Sara.

'I won't leave you.'

It will be our last time together. At least I can comfort her when she wakes.

Jenny kisses her on the forehead; Sara moves, groans and whispers, 'Help me.'

Sara repeats the plea a few seconds later: louder, more urgent. 'Help me.'

Jenny is in torment. She came to rescue Sara but doesn't know how. What about the lady with white curly hair that Sara sent to visit her? Where is she?

That woman was free to move around – she must be downstairs.

Jenny climbs from the bed and finds her dressing gown. 'Stay calm, Sara. I'm going to find that woman you sent. She can help us.'

The corridor is still empty. Directly across is an alcove with chairs and a door. She turns the handle: it's locked. The only other option is at the end if the corridor. Jenny shuffles towards it with dwindling hopes. She's been there before, but Nancy's swipe card was required. She keeps walking.

As she gets nearer, Jenny realises the door is not quite closed. She pushes it carefully. It opens slowly with a hissing noise and she enters a large space so bright and confusing it makes her dizzy. She holds onto the wall and sees a sink, mop and buckets. The floor is shiny, smooth and cold. Stars are visible through a window near the ceiling.

There are more rooms in the distance. She tries to get her bearings but hears heavy footsteps. She crouches in a corner behind the cleaning equipment. It's Harry again. He's pre-occupied by something in his hands.

Jenny is terrified he will find her within seconds. He'll drag her back to her room and drug her again.

I'll never be able to save Sara.

He turns before reaching Jenny. He unlocks a door, stands on the threshold for a few seconds and then goes back the way he came, leaving the door half open.

CHAPTER 45

Meg

I'M CALMER, THANKS TO MY YEARS OF READING THE STOICS. THE CRITICAL, analytical part of my brain was not going to stop working because my situation was hopeless.

I examined my surroundings, seeking anything that might help me.

I tugged at the straps that bound me to the bed. The restraints had been made for a much larger person than me. There was a bit of wriggle space. I made my right hand as small as possible, pressing my thumb under my palm, and worked my wrist back and forth. It was no use. I couldn't get the angle right and the strap stuck fast against the bone at the base of my thumb. I tried the left side with no better result.

I heard a noise outside the room. I closed my eyes and fearfully listened to the door open. It was Harry – I could smell his peppermint breath. I hoped he thought I was still asleep and wouldn't need to drug me again. There was no movement for a few seconds, then a grunt and I heard him walk away.

I opened my eyes and looked again at the straps. If I twisted my body, lining it up with the strap and pulled directly away from it, I might be able to squeeze my arm out. I pulled with my shoulder, wriggled my wrist and jerked my hand back and forth.

The canvas scraped against the side of my thumb, it felt like bones were dislocating. I kept pulling and jerking, ignoring the pain, but my hand stuck fast. I paused to take a breath and then started again. 'Pull!' But the base of my hand was truly stuck and I couldn't free it.

I groaned, lay back and closed my eyes. I was trapped and wanted to cry.

CHAPTER 46

Jenny

SHE WAITS UNTIL SHE CAN NO LONGER HEAR FOOTSTEPS, THEN SHE STUMBLES to the door that Harry left open. It's her only option. It's gloomy inside, there's movement, a groan. Jenny backs out into the brightness.

She is frightened, confused. Jenny needs help, but she is the one supposed to be saving Sara. She hears crying in the dark space. It is another resident at the mercy of Harry? Jenny can't stand there, he might return. She moves to the frame and looks inside, waiting for her eyes to adjust.

A machine blinks next to a bed with someone in it. She hears her name.

'Jenny!'

CHAPTER 47

Meg

I OPENED MY EYES AND SAW AN ANGEL. SHE WAS TALL, DRESSED IN WHITE; her feet were bare, and her reddish grey hair flowed down to her shoulders. We stared at each other; me trapped, her about to take flight. Until I recognised her.

'Jenny!' She halted. 'Jenny, please.'

Cautiously she entered my room and stopped at the end of the bed.

'I need you to help me, Jenny, please.' I didn't know how she found me, but I didn't care. I had to break through the fog of drugs that had turned her into a zombie.

'I'm Meg. Remember me? I'm a friend of Sara.'

That sparked a reaction. 'I must rescue Sara.' Jenny turned to leave.

'Don't go,' I cried. 'I can help you. We can rescue her together.'

She paused and then moved closer to my face. I was still wearing the mask; all she could see were my eyes.

'You came to see me. You're the woman Sara sent.'

'Yes. Help me get out of these straps and we can find help.'

She stepped back, once more ready to flee. 'Not that man.'

'No. I have friends, Lila and Dorothy. We'll contact them and they will rescue Sara. They will save us from that man.' I jiggled the restraints. 'First, you need to unbuckle this strap?'

She stared at me for a few more seconds, then acted. Her fingers were surprisingly nimble and strong. I was soon free and able to sit up.

That was a mistake. I grabbed the metal arm of the bed to control a dizzy spell passed. Jenny waited patiently. I slid to the side of the bed, turned sideways so that I could balance against it as I put my feet on the floor.

My knees were weak but I was able to stand while holding onto the bed. The mask was blocking off my vision so I took it off. I was wearing a pair of blue pyjamas that the nurses must have taken from my room. There was no sign of my slippers or any other footwear. Josephine and Deidre never wanted me to leave that bed – except in a coffin.

I fought for balance as I crossed the room. Jenny offered support.

'Let's walk together' Arm in arm we circled the room to steady our legs and decide what to do.

Each small lap made me stronger, but I was also having qualms about that Jenny had placed all her trust in me. She believed I could help Sara. I knew that our chances were slim; my own escape had been thwarted by Deidre and Harry. They were still running Sunnyvale like a prison. We had to find a way out of the hospital wing, get out of the main building and work out how to contact Lila and Dorothy. The challenges made my legs wobbly again. Jenny stopped me from falling and gave me a questioning look.

There's no going back. We must give it a try.

'Let's go,' I said.

Outside the door was an empty space, almost unbearably bright after the dimness within my room. I looked both ways. No one was in sight. Closed doors stretched away into the distance on either side of the hallway. A line of windows close to the ceiling revealed it was night. I had no idea how long I'd been held captive.

We moved arm in arm to the end of the hall. I held my breath as we rounded the corner into a reception area with carpet underfoot. Our luck was getting better; there was a narrow elevator. I pressed the button. Relief welled as a motor behind the door indicated would soon be at our feet.

'Ladies!' A nurse rushed from an office. Her uniform was dishevelled, perhaps she had been asleep. Her face showed alarm as she approached.

'You shouldn't be here. We're in lockdown – go back to your rooms right now.' It looked like she meant to take us back by force. But she stopped a few metres away, then retreated a few steps.

'Mrs Thorne, don't you realise how serious this is? You've got the virus and you could infect everyone. You must go back to your bed. And Mrs Mueller, what will Mrs Wakefield say?'

Jenny quailed and dropped my arm.

I wasn't sick. Josephine and Deidre had falsely spread the story that I had Covid 19 to isolate me. They were going to murder me and sneak my body out with real victims of the coronavirus. The staff didn't know they had nothing to fear from being close to me. I could use that trepidation.

The lift door opened, I grabbed Jenny's arm and swung inside. The nurse was too scared to follow us. She took out her phone and watched the doors close. We held each other tightly as the lift descended. One obstacle had been overcome. There would be more.

We emerged near the ground floor reception. Yvonne, the night nurse, stepped out of the office holding her mobile.

'They're here,' she said.

I saw a cleaner walking towards us from the common room, a nurse's aide approached from the other corridor.

A fever and a dry cough were the main symptoms of Covid-19, according to the television reports.

I coughed noisily into my free hand and held it front of me. I must have looked like that horrifying Hollywood scene of Boris Karloff in the *The Mummy*. The effect we had was much the same. Yvonne backed off, the aide came to a wary halt many metres away and the cleaner decided she wasn't paid for this. She ran away.

The agitated nurse from upstairs arrived on the scene. 'I don't know what happened. Jenny Mueller must have helped Mrs Thorne get out of her room. We have to find Harry. He has the right gear. Better contact Mrs Wakefield and Deidre.'

'Harry's gone home,' said Yvonne. 'Deidre's on her way. She'll take care of the problem. We shouldn't disturb Mrs Wakefield. Not yet.'

It was no good trying to get out the front door. I pulled Jenny around and we supported each other as we walked slowly away from reception. From time to time I coughed into my hand and extended my arm. The nurses followed at a distance.

They went from threatening us, to cajoling and finally to pleading.

My theatrics convinced them it wasn't healthy to physically stop us. We ignored them. I knew there was an emergency exit around the next corner. Hauling ourselves the last few metres made me think of *The Mummy again;* each step we took together was slow and laborious.

Jenny's pace quickened when she saw the red sign.

The pack behind us was growing; there were more voices. Had Deidre joined the pursuit? She knew I wasn't infected with the virus. I could almost feel her hand on my shoulder. The red light loomed above us, my extended arm hit the release bar. It didn't budge.

I let go of Jenny and pushed with both arms. It still wouldn't open. They couldn't lock it — that was illegal. I put all my frail weight on the bar, pushing forward with both feet. The heavy door opened a fraction, a burst of fresh air. Jenny was straining as well, neither of us had time to see if the nurses would summon the courage to prevent a covid case escaping.

The door suddenly swung open, we always pitched onto the concrete. I grabbed the frame, righted myself, and then Jenny took my arm and we scampered away from the main building.

We reached the driveway. An alarm boomed behind us, ahead light filtered through trees in the park. It was almost dawn. The air was surprisingly warm and a gentle breeze brushed my cheek. Jenny gasped. I wondered how long since she had experienced a sunrise.

I had to suppress feelings of joy. We were out. But we weren't free.

The nurses hadn't abandoned their pursuit. One circled around to block the driveway, another moved to the side to hem us between the building and the wall.

'Close the gate,' Yvonne yelled. She was the closest, about five metres away. The nurse aide reached the gate, then fell back as a car sped through the entrance. Deidre climbed out; her hair was a mess and the sweatshirt and baggy trousers were far from a professional uniform.

She tried to make me cower with a steely gaze, then she saw Jenny and reeled back. The manager who acted more like a prison camp commandant was apprehensive. She turned her anger on the nursing staff.

'What imbecile allowed this to happen?'

The upstairs nurse quailed.

Then she turned to me. In the growing light I could see a mixture of fear and anger in her face.

'What do you think you are doing, Mrs Thorne? You are causing lot of trouble and you've put Jenny Mueller in danger. Mrs Wakefield will be appalled. What will she say when she finds out that Jenny has been exposed to this virus because of you?'

I think she was more concerned about Josephine Wakefield's reaction than our welfare.

She turned to Jenny, her voice softening. 'You've been very foolish, Jenny, but no one is going to punish you. Your aunt will be so worried about you. You know how much you are hurting her. You need to come back inside where you will be safe. Leave that woman, turn around and go with Yvonne. Look, she is holding the door open for you.'

Deidre Barr was trying to assume the manner of someone speaking gently to a confused old woman. Her words weren't coming out that way. Jenny quailed and backed away.

'You're a criminal,' I croaked. 'And Jenny remembers what Josephine did.'

Deidre looked like she didn't know whether to laugh at me or curse. She turned to the group surrounding us. 'The fever is affecting her mind. She's so far gone that she's suffering from delusions. If we want to save her, we have to get her inside as quickly as possible.' The staff didn't say anything. 'I'll get into my protective gear. She pointed at the upstairs nurse. 'You close the gate.'

The woman scurried to obey her manager's command only to be forced aside by the arrival of a white van. It halted behind Deidre's car. It had a large blue sign on the window: Covid-19 Emergency Response Team. Beside it was the coat of arms of Victoria.

CHAPTER 48

Meg

TWO FIGURES EMERGED FROM THE VAN WRAPPED HEAD TO FEET IN WHITE plastic, their faces covered with masks and goggles. One was short and squat, the other was a head taller and broader in the shoulders. The tall one strode up to Deidre, turned on a small, checked her clip board. 'Are you the supervisor of this establishment?'

'Who are you?'

She pointed at the van sign. 'I think that's obvious. We have orders to collect one of your residents.' She looked at the page. 'Margaret Thorne is reported to have Covid-19. She had to be isolated immediately at the Royal Melbourne Hospital.'

The other masked person pointed a gloved finger at me and Jenny. 'Who are these women standing outside in their night clothes?'

The relief almost made me collapse. It was Lila and Dorothy. But their disguises weren't going to last long in the rising sun. Lila walked closer and could see she was wearing ski goggles and a voluminous rain cape.

'This woman looks very ill. What is she doing outside in the cold in such a state? And why did you allow this other woman to accompany her. Don't you know that we're in the middle of a pandemic?'

'I'm Meg. Margaret Thorne,' I said feebly, and coughed. 'And this is Jenny Mueller.' Jenny coughed too.

Deidre strode up to Lila. 'This woman has unfortunately wandered from her room, and somehow enticed Mrs Mueller to accompany her. I am about to put on my protective equipment so I can escort them back inside. I can assure you that we are able to care for them. We have fulfilled all the requirements of the Commission on Aged Care and have the necessary equipment at hand to deal with the virus.'

Dorothy looked up from her clipboard and addressed the whole group. 'Your assurance is not good enough. Our unit was formed by the government for the purpose of ensuring that citizens who get Covid receive the best possible treatment, that health workers are protected and the public is safe from infection.' She recited this in the weary voice of an overworked public servant.

She looked back at her clipboard. 'We have reason to believe that Margaret Thorne is not being adequately monitored and treated for a disease that is particularly serious in the elderly, and that other residents and staff in this facility are not sufficiently protected from infection. The fact that Mrs Thorne is wandering around outside with another resident is reason enough to believe that your standard of care is deficient.'

'Who told you to come?' Deidre glared at the fake nurses.

Dorothy shook her head. 'We are not at liberty to divulge that information. The emergency powers given to us by the government give us unlimited authority to act whenever there is any reason for alarm. Failure to comply with our directives will result in a serious fine and perhaps a jail term.'

Lila was now by my side. She reached inside her cape, pulled out a rectangular device and held the nozzle next to my forehead. She took it away and squinted at it. 'Thirty-eight point five. She's running a fever. We have to get her to hospital.' She hesitated. 'The other woman, Mrs Mueller, is probably infected too. She must also come with us.'

The sun appeared over the trees and we could see each other more clearly. Deidre, ignoring requirements of social distancing, rushed to Lila, barring the way between us and the van.

'I know you. I've seen you at Sunnyvale.' She pointed her finger at Lila and then swung round to Dorothy. 'And I know you too. You're that woman who used to work for us.' She turned to the nurses who were huddled in a group a long distance from the rest of us. 'This is a sham. They're trying to kidnap our residents. They're trying to take away Mrs Wakefield's niece. Stop them. Shut the gate. I've called the police. They'll soon be here.'

But Deidre's staff didn't move.

Dorothy raised her chin and turned to the nurses.

'Yes, I worked here. Now I'm proud to be in the Emergency Response Unit. All of us need to think of how we can protect each other during these difficult times.' She sound authoritative and weary, as if she had been working non-stop. 'But I can't say I am surprised that we were called here. I saw how unsatisfactory conditions are, especially upstairs. It's not a safe place for a sick people – or staff.'

'Look at them,' Deidre pointed at Dorothy and Lila. 'Look at that van.' The vehicle was clean, but there was a deep scratch along the side of the door, scrapes on the bumper and rust on the tyre rims.

'As you've heard on the news,' said Dorothy, 'proper equipment is scarce. We've had to improvise as best we can.'

'Where are your masks?' Lila asked the nurses. 'Where is your protective gear?'

She was moving Jenny and me towards the back of the van. Deidre ran to intercept us. I did some more coughing and Jenny joined me, but this time it didn't work. Deidre grabbed at Jenny.

Suddenly Dorothy was by our side. Deidre struck out, but Dorothy easily deflected the blow and shunted Deidre against the van.

I've phoned the police,' she said. 'You'll be sorry.'

Deidre would have also phoned Harry. He wouldn't be far away.

Dorothy saw me shiver. 'Don't worry,' she whispered. 'The real ambulance will soon be here. I phoned Sara's son too. He's not going to stand by and do nothing.'

A siren sounded from the street. A police car drove up pulled in beside the van. Two officers emerged and put on their caps.

Deidre stepped forward. 'I'm the manager of Sunnyvale and that woman assaulted me.' She pointed at Dorothy. 'Arrest her.'

The police nodded; one tapped the van. 'What's this?' Dorothy waved her clipboard.

'We're the Covid-19 Emergency Response Unit and these two women need to be taken into isolation.'

'Never heard of such a thing,' said the other police officer. But he seemed unsure.

'They're trespassers,' screamed Deidre, 'and they're trying to abduct residents.'

Another alarm could be heard approaching. A few seconds later an ambulance joined the parking lot. Two paramedics in yellow vests got out. 'Where's the patient?'

'She's upstairs,' I croaked. 'Her name is Sara Brighouse.'

I turned to Jenny who was still beside me. 'If they take her to the hospital, she'll be safe.'

'Wait a moment,' said the first police officer. 'Who called an ambulance?'

Dorothy raised her hand. 'It seems clear to me that this situation is an emergency. People can die because of the Sunnyvale's incompetence.'

'Do you have authorisation to make that judgment?' The policeman was looking at the sign on the van window.

The paramedics were confused. They were waiting for clear directions.

Deidre, sensing that she could get the police on her side, pushed her case. 'They don't have proper equipment. Look at that van.'

One of the police officers did. Its shoddiness was even more apparent in the morning light. He kicked the front tyre and addressed Lila. 'Is this thing safe to drive?'

'Proper equipment is scarce,' repeated Dorothy wearily, 'as you've probably heard on the news. We're using what we can get.'

Deidre turned to the paramedics. 'You don't need to be here. Everyone inside is safe.'

But they didn't move.

Lila pulled on my arm, encouraging me to move towards the back of the van. I tried to get Jenny to follow, but she refused.

'Sara,' she said. 'We can't leave without Sara.'

I turned to Lila. 'Jenny helped me get away so we could rescue Sara Brighouse.' My voice was hoarse.

'Please Meg. We must get you loaded so that we can get away from here when we have a chance.'

The police were staring at us doubtfully. 'Are you authorised to enter these grounds and take residents away?'

'They're trespassers and kidnappers,' repeated Deidre.

I felt the situation was slipping beyond us. Would the police send

Jenny and I back inside and arrest Lila and Dorothy? They were our rescuers; the real criminal was standing in front of them.

Another car added to the confusion in the driveway. Mr Brighouse emerged angrily, wearing a hastily donned overcoat. 'What's happening to my mother? I demand to see her.'

'Your mother,' said Deidre, 'is in the hospital ward and I assure you she is fine.'

'Does she have Covid?'

'She is being treated.'

'I want to see her. I'm told she needs emergency treatment.' He began striding towards the building. Yvonne fell into step with him, the paramedics followed.

Deidre was more worried about Jenny and I escaping. 'Don't let them get away.'

But the police had obviously decided to wait until Mr Brighouse and the paramedics emerged from the building.

Lila pulled at my arm. 'Let's go.'

The tap of a cane could be heard on concrete. Josephine Wakefield arrived on the scene with imperial grandeur.

'What is the trouble here?' She saw Jenny standing beside me.

'What are you doing out in the cold?' She grabbed her by the shoulder. 'Bad girl.'

Jenny flinched and drew away. I stepped between them. 'Jenny needs help and she wants to be taken to a place where she can be safe.'

'No,' Josephine was agitated, but still in control. 'This is my house. She is my daughter and I have the right to care for her.'

The police seemed moved by a mother's appeal. One put his arm on Jenny's back. 'Be a good girl. Go with your mother.'

Jenny pulled back. 'No!' she screamed

'Jenny, come back inside with me.' It was a command, not a mother's request.

'I won't,' Jenny moved back to my side.

'She shouldn't be forced to go where she doesn't want to go,' I said. I turned to Jenny. 'Do you want to come with us?'

Jenny nodded.

'No, I forbid it.' said Josephine.

Lila was already helping Jenny to into the van.

At that moment, the paramedics returned with Sara Brighouse. Her son walked beside the stretcher, holding her hand. He looked up at Dorothy as he passed. 'Thank you for calling me, Mrs Arden.'

Lila opened the back of van. 'Quick. Get in.'

The interior smelled of dog. There was a single bed mattress spread out on the floor covered with a freshly ironed sheet. A blanket was lying on top and a folded stretcher lay alongside.

'You two will have to huddle together,' said Lila as she helped me inside beside Jenny.

'Do I really have a fever?' I asked her.

'If you do, my hairdryer won't tell us.'

From the window I could see that Sara had been put into the ambulance and Mr Brighouse and Dorothy were talking to the police.

Lila got into the driver's seat and started the motor.

'Hold onto each other,' she said. 'We're on our way.'

CHAPTER 49

Meg

'Are we going to hospital?' I asked.

'Are you ill?'

'I don't know.' I was feeling terribly tired. My throat was sore and I wasn't sure the coughing was a sham.

'Best go to my place,' said Lila. 'I can phone Jenny's son from there and I can keep an eye on you. We'll have to be safe and keep you isolated. You can use my bedroom. It has an attached bathroom and I can use the rest of the house. Colin will see that his mother gets proper care.'

'What about Dorothy?'

'She'll join us – if she doesn't end up in jail. We broke a few laws to rescue you.'

'Much obliged,' I managed to say.

I lay down and put my arms around Jenny, and worried though I was about Dorothy and Sara, I soon lost consciousness.

Lila woke us up, helped us out of the van, and guided us through a gate, down a corridor and into the heart of a sprawling Edwardian house. Jenny was supporting me. I got a fleeting impressions of a long narrow hallway lined with doors, one leading to a bedroom with a neatly made four poster bed, a lounge full of old furniture, a mantelpiece with family pictures and then a large comfortable kitchen – the room where the Galli family and their guests had congregated for meals and conversation.

Lila sat us down at one end of a long table and made us a cup of tea. As she boiled the kettle she shed her mask and the plastic layers. 'I can't be sure you don't have the virus, so we need to stay a safe distance.' She sat at the other end.

The tea was terrible but it made me feel better. 'How did you know to come?'

'Your sweetheart, that bloke Miles Reading, contacted Dorothy. He must have got her number from the office records. He was worried about you. He said you had been taken up to the floor where they put dementia and hospital cases.'

'He's not my sweetheart.'

How had he had managed to do this in lockdown? But I already knew that he had a talent for surveillance and subterfuge. I wouldn't be surprised to learn that he could pick locks.

Lila shrugged. 'We couldn't visit Sunnyvale because of the lockdown. And of course, we didn't get anywhere when we rang them up. They just told us you might have been exposed to the coronavirus and were being properly looked after. I rang the police and someone on the Aged Care Commission, but they wrote me off as an overwrought relative. They had their hands full dealing with cases and policing emergency measures. Maybe they called Sunnyvale and got the same run around. Anyway, they didn't see any reason to investigate. We had to take matters into our own hands. We planned our raid for early in the morning before people on the day shift arrived. We thought we'd be better off if we didn't encounter Deidre.'

'Do you think she called the police?' I asked. I looked around uneasily. Perhaps at any moment they would arrive in force to take us back. Perhaps Josephine Wakefield would come with a posse to capture Jenny.

'I doubt Deidre would dare. It was clear she'd lost the support of her staff. Anyway, Dorothy will have a lot to tell them if they come. We spent yesterday and most of the night preparing. The rain capes were easy to find but we had to borrow the goggles from my sister. Her grandkids go skiing. Masks are pretty much unavailable in the shops just now, but we improvised. And the gloves came from the kitchen. We got my brother George to clean his van. My nephew is an artist and he made the sign. The mattress came from my spare room, and we got a stretcher from a bloke in my street who used to do first aid training.'

'How were you going to get us out?'

'We were going to ring the bell, and demand to be taken up to your ward. We were going to take you out on the stretcher. But we wouldn't have bothered if we'd known you were going to rescue yourself.'

'It was really Jenny who rescued me.'

Jenny was bent over her teacup, almost asleep.

'We'll put her in the bed in the back room and I'll call her son,' said Lila. 'She can stay there until he decides what to do. You can use the same room.'

I put my hand on Jenny's shoulder and she raised her head. 'Is Sara here yet?'

'She's going to hospital,' said Lila. 'When you wake up we'll be able to tell you about her.'

We went together to Lila's spare bedroom. Jenny lay down and instantly fell asleep. I covered her with a quilt. I felt like lying down beside her but I decided that I'd better tell Lila everything I knew, just in case I had been exposed to the virus. I also had to make sure that Dorothy was safe.

When I got back to the kitchen Lila gave me another cup of the awful tea. She had just put it down in front of me when her phone rang.

'Dorothy is fine,' she waved her arm with relief. 'The police let her go. They're puzzled about the van but they figure that there *could* be a newly created Covid-19 Emergency Response Unit with special powers given to it by the government. Dorothy can be persuasive. Anyway, she'll be here soon in a taxi.'

I began my narrative while I was still alert enough to tell the story. 'I had to leave behind Jenny's letter,' I told Lila when I finished. 'I had no choice.'

'Not to worry, said Lila. 'Now that Jenny is out of Sunnyvale, I think she'll be able to speak for herself. I'll talk to Mr Brighouse and Mr Mueller this morning. I'm sure they will get their lawyers on to the case. They're the best people to call the police.'

We both startled when we heard the doorbell. Lila brought Dorothy into the room and poured her out a cup of tea.

'Sara's in hospital,' Dorothy told us. 'Her son is there too, but she's in isolation. He can't see her until she's tested.'

I was no longer able to keep awake. Lila found me a nightdress.

'I hope you don't mind sharing the bed with Jenny for now. We can get you everything you need later.'

Unconcerned that the nightie was like a tent and I couldn't brush my teeth, I fell into bed beside Jenny who did not wake when I moved under the quilt beside her.

I woke up briefly when Lila entered and helped Jenny out of bed.

'Your son is here to take you home,' said Lila.

'Sara?' asked Jenny.

'She's safe.'

I went back to sleep. It was the next morning before I felt strong enough to dress in clothes Dorothy had collected from my flat. The tea was another matter. I asked Lila to get me an electric jug and a packet of Earl Grey.

'I'm happy to make you cups of tea or coffee whenever you want them.'

'I hate to tell you this, but you make dreadful tea. Some people are simply incapable of making a good cup.' I laughed. 'It's a form of disability.'

'Whinging pom!'

A few hours later I opened the door to find a new tea set. A China teapot decorated with red roses beside matching cups. There was a milk jug, packet of tea and a strainer. Beside them was an electric jug.

'I thought,' said Lila 'that roses were appropriate for you. Those who admire them don't think of the thorns until they try to grab them by their stems.'

With a good cup of tea at my side I rang the number forwarded to me by Dorothy.

'Miles, I'm safe, how are you?'

Everyone downstairs was well, he told me, although they were allowed to walk the courtyard one by one. 'It's like being in prison. Worse.'

He told me that the police had visited and Deidre had disappeared. Arrested, he hoped. He hadn't heard anything about Josephine Wakefield. He would see what he could do about the tea canister, but he suspected it had already been removed by the police.

'Stay safe.'

'Yes. You too.'

Lila was not allowed to visit Dan. She moped around the house wondering whether her absence was making him suffer, worrying about whether he would survive the pandemic. 'He's got all sorts of conditions. And look at what's happening in institutions overseas.' She was on the phone every day to a nurse at the hospice.

Lila and Colin Mueller also spoke to each other every day. He had been given Jenny's letter by the police. But Jenny was able to tell her own story now she was off the drug that had dulled her mind.

Both Jenny and Sara had tested negative for Covid-19 and their sons were looking after them.

'So that was all a lie,' I said to Lila. I felt lighter. A burden had been lifted from my shoulders. Now that I had recovered from the drugs they had given me, I felt well. There was no need for me to get tested.

CHAPTER 50

Meg

A WEEK AFTER I GOT OUT OF SUNNYVALE, THE POLICE INTERVIEWED ME. IT had to be done remotely. A technician came in a mask and gloves to set up the equipment in Lila's back bedroom.

I was pleased that the interviewer was a woman. She wanted to know about the persecution of Sara Brighouse and why I thought Deidre was responsible. I started telling her about my meeting with Simon Long and his investigation of the finances of Sunnyvale. She cut me off.

'He and Deidre Barr are also being interviewed,' she said. She would come back to me later if necessary.

She was also not interested in my suspicions about Martin Wilde, or about Jenny's letter or what I overheard when I was strapped in the bed upstairs at Sunnyvale.

'We are investigating all these matters,' she said. I think she believed I'd been hallucinating. She was clearly impressed and even amused by the story of my escape. But then she rocked me.

'Your friends broke the law.'

I felt deflated when she terminated the interview.

According to Colin Mueller's lawyer, Deidre admitted receiving under-the-counter payments from Josephine Wakefield. She *assumed* it was a reward for being a good employee. She denied persecuting Sara or threatening to kill Jenny and me. The allegations were the delusional fantasy of a crazy old woman who had always disliked her. She conceded to perhaps treating me roughly, but she said I tended to wander. As a suspected Covid-19 case I had to be restrained for everyone's safety. Martin Wilde, I also heard, had denied any wrongdoing.

The interview and these reports made me despair. Perhaps Deidre would be charged with fraud or at least tax evasion, but what was done to Jenny and Sara was likely to go unpunished, and no one was going to take seriously my account of the conversation between Josephine and Deidre.

Jenny was strong enough to make a statement about the murder of her mother. Dorothy said people with mental disabilities can be interviewed if they understand what it means to tell the truth. But I didn't think the police would be prepared to prosecute based on a statement of a woman suffering from dementia, especially when the crime happened many years ago. Mrs Wakefield was likely to remain untouchable and so was Wilde. Even worse, it looked like the board of Sunnyvale might prosecute Dorothy and Lila for trespass and other misdemeanours.

I didn't know about the persistence of Colin Mueller. He hired an investigator who was able to locate Rosalind Parker: Rosie, the woman who had once cared for Jenny. She was seriously ill with lung cancer but willing to talk. He was able to get Rosie to admit that she was an accomplice in the murder of Jenny's mother. It was shocking to listen to a recording of their conversation.

'Mrs Wakefield told me she was going to confront her sister-in-law and that I should take Jenny to the park for an hour and then bring her to her house.' Rosalind's voice was hoarse. 'She said she would solve my problem. I wouldn't have to go to prison,'

When asked why Jenny's mother threatened her with prison, Rosie said it was because she had stolen something.

'I didn't really think she would kill her sister-in-law. I just thought she would threaten her. It was only when Jenny told me what she saw that I knew, but I had to do what Mrs Wakefield said if I didn't want to get into real trouble. She said I would be a suspect. She said they wouldn't believe me if I told on her. I am sure that's true. Then she told me to get rid of the clothes she was wearing when she did the murder. There was blood on them. I did what she asked. But that was all. Afterwards she gave me some money and told me to leave and never see Jenny again.'

Rosie was weeping by the end of her confession.

Sara became more coherent once she was able to communicate with Jenny again. She said Deidre told her that Jenny would suffer if she revealed the Wakefield family secret. Mr Brighouse told us he intended to sue Sunnyvale for criminal negligence.

We heard nothing more about Lila and Dorothy being charged for trespass or kidnap.

Simon Long's investigation of Sunnyvale's finances were helped by my tip off about Wilde. He examined the donations given to Mrs Wakefield's foundation and found a cluster came from Sunnyvale. Most of these turned out to be the result of Wilde's persuasive powers. When his methods of manipulation were revealed, relatives, and some of residents themselves, consulted their lawyers. Long is an obnoxious man but he was persistent and thorough, and his investigation led to articles in the press about exploitation of elderly people at Sunnyvale.

It was Deidre Barr who cracked first. She didn't want to bear all the blame for the way Jenny and Sara were treated. Nor did she wish to be known as Wilde's accomplice. She confessed to helping Mrs Wakefield deal with Jenny by moving her without good reason to the dementia ward. Deidre claimed Jenny became uncontrollable, hurling accusations about Mrs Wakefield, and had to be sedated. She admitted threatening Sara and drugging and restraining me. Deidre said she was never serious about her threats to get rid of Sara and me. Anything Deidre did at Sunnyvale was under the direction of Mrs Wakefield and for her purposes.

'That woman has no moral compass,' said Dorothy.

'She's a psychopath,' said Lila.

I wondered how many people like that were employed in institutions caring for vulnerable people.

When faced with Deidre's confession, Jospehine Wakefield did not attempt to deny her role. She defended her efforts to milk Sunnyvale residents of donations for her new geriatric centre by saying it was for the good of elderly people. I could visualise her facing her accusers without any sign of remorse: straight backed, queenly, defiant.

The justified the murder of her sister-in-law. She said Elizabeth was a parasite on her family and society. All she wanted from life was a good time, and then she had the idea of marrying a no-good musician and grabbing her part of the inheritance. That would have been the end of the business that her husband had managed so successfully. It would have ruined her own social ambitions and charitable foundation.

The police viewed it differently and charged her with murder.

'I'm glad judges and juries don't let people off for reasons like that,' said Lila. 'Where would we be?'

Dorothy shook her head. 'She must be a Christian. How can she possibly suppose that her good deeds make up for her sins?'

I was sorry that I wasn't still teaching ethics. I could get my students to critically discuss her justification for murder and extortion.

CHAPTER 51

Meg

It is almost a month since Rosie Parker's confession, and I'm back in my flat. Lila was reluctant to let me go and phones every day to see how I am and Dorothy has twice left homemade cakes on my doorstep. I think they are feeling guilty about putting pressure on me to become a resident of Sunnyvale when I didn't want to go. They fear I might have been traumatised by what happened there. Lila keeps asking me if I am having bad dreams.

"What doesn't kill you makes you strong". In my case I think Nietzsche was right. I was frightened, I thought that I was going to die but I not only survived, I learned that I was more resilient and resourceful than I had supposed. I believe that a person has core characteristics and ways of responding to the world that they do not easily lose whatever happens to them. My mother never lost her love for me even when she began to confuse me with her sister. I could tell by the look she gave me when I came into her room. I now know that the determination to do the right thing, and not to give up, are core characteristics of mine. Realising this has made me less apprehensive about old age and less frightened about what will happen to me, though I still have a perfectly rational desire to avoid being put in a nursing home.

Georgia has kept me up to date about life at Sunnyvale. Not

surprisingly, there have been big changes in the management, but most of the residents have stayed.

Miles Reading is an exception. He left the home under the condition that he self-isolate for fourteen days in the house of his brother. As it turned out, his family had not abandoned him. He was the one responsible for his own exile. He now has a flat not far from where I live.

Vera rang to tell me that my philosophy talks had helped her enormously. She is losing weight and has lots of plans to enjoy life with Catherine when the coronavirus restrictions end.

'A new start is always possible. Look at you and Miles.'

I wondered what on earth she was thinking.

Georgia sent photos of her recent paintings. Her subject is now her room and the view from the window.

'Like Grace Cossington Smith though of course I'm not nearly so good.'

She told me that Miles would deliver the pictures I had chosen. 'You took them voluntarily,' she said. 'They're yours for life.'

Wanda wrote to apologise for her reaction to my appearance at her door. She was frightened and anxious. 'But I am not so worried now.' The episode had given her an idea for an adult story – *The Knock at the Door.*

Sometimes Jenny and I communicate via Skype, with Colin's help. She is living with his family. Now that she's off medication, she doesn't show many signs of dementia.

'I do forget the simplest things,' she told me. 'I don't know how to get to the shops, and yesterday I forgot that I put a kettle on the stove, but Colin says he'll find someone to take care of me when he and his wife are no longer working from home.'

Lila is now reading chapters of *Middlemarch* into a recorder and sending them to Saint Bernard's where they can be played near Dan's bedside. She's been sending me copies, perhaps with the idea that I can play them if I have bad dreams or trouble going to sleep. She has a melodious reading voice and I often listen to them even though nightmares and insomnia are not my problems. James Melling died, but not before he made a statement to Lila's lawyer, who thinks there's a good chance the school will be pay a significant sum into a trust fund for Dan.

In the mornings, Miles goes to the cemetery to visit the graves of his wife and grandchildren. For a while it looked like the government was going to put cemeteries out of bounds, but fortunately they abandoned the idea. In the afternoons, he visits me. To avoid social isolation during this time of Covid, single people can have one visitor providing it is always the same person. Miles and I find it convenient and congenial to take advantage of this permission to have a chat and a cup of tea together. We sit socially distanced in the lounge room and drink tea out of my rose-painted cups. Sometimes he tells me about his experiences as a hydrologist working on dam projects around the country. He has a wry, self-deprecating sense of humour. But mostly we don't talk. We watch the blackbirds flitting about in my neighbour's garden. The leaves on their trees are turning brown. Winter will soon be here.

'Covid restrictions are a real problem for a courtship,' said Lila.

'Wait to get married until all the restrictions have ended,' said Dorothy. 'Then we can have a proper celebration in the Gardener's Arms. I'll organise it.'

I explain once again that there is no courtship and there will be no marriage. Miles and I are merely friends.

Just the same, I sometimes imagine that we might get a place together when the pandemic is over. If it has two entrances and separate living areas, then we can have as much or as little to do with each other as we like. Perhaps it will also have a veranda on three sides.

But who knows how the crisis will end or what will happen to us? Perhaps we will not survive it.

As the stoic Marcus Aurelius said: "Concentrate on appreciating what exists and do not concern yourself with a future that you may never experience."

JANNA THOMPSON

Janna Thompson, one of Australia's most distinguished philosophers, was also a devoted fan of crime fiction and a long-time member of Sisters in Crime Australia. When the pandemic hit Melbourne in 2020, she was inspired to try her hand at crime writing.

The result is *Lockdown*, a novel which explores how the invisibility of older women can provide the perfect cover for criminal investigations. No one would suspect that a retired philosophy professor, who is prone to wearing pastels, would be on the track of undercovering wrong doing.

As a student in Minnesota, USA, Janna worked on the local paper which taught her how to write direct and engaging prose. She had initially thought to train as a journalist but decided to throw her lot in with philosophy.

After a stint at Manchester University, she migrated to Australia in 1970 and taught at Monash University and then La Trobe University, where she became a professor. She published five books and gained an international reputation, particularly in the field of historical reparations. She also joined the Communist Party of Australia and remained a member until it dissolved in 1991.

Janna was also an avid cyclist, canoeist, bush walker, cross-country skier, and swimmer. She once rode a camel across a desert in India. She died in June 2022, only a few months after being diagnosed with multiple brain tumours. One of her last missions was to arrange for the publication of *Lockdown*.

She never wore pastels.

Lightning Source UK Ltd.
Milton Keynes UK
UKHW040911060323
418105UK00005B/585